Roger Pulvers is an author, playwright, theater director, translator and filmmaker. He has published more than fifty books in Japanese and English, including novels, essays, plays, and poetry. Working as assistant to director Nagisa Oshima on *Merry Christmas, Mr. Lawrence* brought him back to Japan and inspired him to become the award-winning playwright, film director and prolific author he is today. His novel, *Hoshizuna Monogatari* (*Star Sand*), which he wrote in Japanese, was published by Kodansha, Japan's largest publisher, in 2015, and subsequently in English and French in 2016 and 2017 respectively. It was released as a film, directed by him, in 2017. His most recent books are a novel, *Liv*, and his autobiography, *The Unmaking of an American*, both published by Balestier Press.

ALSO BY ROGER PULVERS

The Dream of Lafcadio Hearn
Liv
The Unmaking of an American
Peaceful Circumstances
The Honey and the Fires

ROGER PULVERS

HALF
of
EACH OTHER

A Novel

BALESTIER PRESS
LONDON · SINGAPORE

Balestier Press
Centurion House, Staines-upon-Thames, London TW18 4AX
www.balestier.com

Half of Each Other

First published by Balestier Press in 2019

A CIP catalogue record for this book
is available from the British Library.

ISBN 978 1 911221 35 7

Cover illustration by Lucy Pulvers

This book is a work of fiction. The literary perceptions and
insights are based on experience, all names, characters, places,
and incidents either are products of the author's imagination
or are used fictitiously.

HALF
of
EACH OTHER

THOUGH MUCH TIME HAS GONE BY I CAN STILL PICTURE A red down jacket hanging off the severed branch of a tree. It is a cherry blossom tree, and it is in full bloom, but the petals are colorless. The only true color in this picture comes from the jacket, a stroke of red ink hastily brushed on a matted gray canvas.

The jacket belonged to me, and the person standing in the cherry blossom tree's shade is my father, Nicholas York. He is absolutely still for the moment, a statue of his own invention.

You see, my daddy is a spulc-tor. I can't pronounce that word very well even now, but I know what it means because I have seen him making his little statues of people out of clay. I think there will be many spulc-tors in the world because all of the little children at my kindergarten made statues out of clay like daddy's.

There is another person not far away. She is my mummy, Setsuko York, and she is at the very edge of the picture. Daddy doesn't know she's there. But first let me tell you how they happened to be there.

THE CHERRY BLOSSOM TREE STANDS IN FRONT OF MY kindergarten. Mrs. Katayama has been running it for so long that three generations of people in the neighborhood have gone there. The person who takes me to kindergarten and picks me up every day is daddy. That's because mummy works at Isetan Department Store in Shinjuku and doesn't get home in time. In fact, most of the time she doesn't get home until very late at night, and daddy is the one who shops and cooks dinner for me. It's all right, because the only other thing he does is make statues out of clay, and that doesn't really take up so much time.

Daddy definitely worries too much. He worries that I will not finish my toast and jam and that I won't wear my red jacket when there is a chill in the air. I tell him that I'm not cold, but it doesn't do much good. He says that it's still early spring and that means it's cold. You see, my daddy is Irish. I guess it's cold in spring in Ireland, because he can't seem to get used to being here.

So, even though I won't wear the jacket myself, I let him carry it for me. Then he takes it home on the train and brings it back to the kindergarten in the afternoon. Every time I think about daddy now I see him clutching onto my red down jacket in front of the kindergarten. He is surrounded by Japanese mummies and he bows to them, which looks really funny because he is at least a head taller than all of them.

It makes it easier for me to see him.

EMI IS CONSTANTLY CRITICIZING ME. IMAGINE BEING criticized by a five-year-old. She is never satisfied with anything.

"My bath ready, daddy?" is the first thing she says upon

walking in the door and throwing her cap on the floor. I got her into the habit of taking an early bath. When she's finished she walks through the kitchen with wet feet, a large towel around her body and a smaller one propping up her hair.

"The bath is filthy, daddy," she says. "You'll have to clean it before mummy comes home."

By nine, when she is in bed, I can sit myself at my workbench. Setsuko usually comes home by ten. I wait for her to eat dinner, or, if I am lost in my statues, I do not eat at all.

When my mummy returns home from work she comes into my bedroom without putting her handbag down and stares at me in my bed. Sometimes I sit up and see both my parents staring at me as if I was a strange animal in a zoo. They are not talking to each other. In fact, they rarely talk to each other.

One night I asked them, "Why are you staring at me like that?"

"Because I heard you scream," said my mummy.

"Scream? I didn't scream."

I look at my daddy's hands. There is a big lump of clay sticking off the top of his index finger like a nose on a clown. It really makes me laugh. My parents look at each other. They can't understand why I am laughing. Without saying anything, mummy leaves my room. I can hear her making herself a cup of coffee in the kitchen. Daddy kisses my forehead, tucks me in and smiles at me.

Daddy won a prize a few years ago, before I was born, for his spulc-ture. But now no one wants to buy it. I know that he is not happy, but he says he is happy because of me. It's not enough to be happy because of me.

We were on a crowded train, traveling from Seijo Gakuenmae Station to Kyodo Station. My kindergarten was a long walk from Kyodo Station. He claimed that it was a short walk, but his opinion was wrong.

"It takes us eight minutes and thirty seconds, approximately, to get from the station to the kindergarten," I explained to him on several occasions, "and that, by Japanese standards, whether you are aware of it or not, is a long time to walk anywhere, daddy."

He gazed down at me and frowned, trying to slip his hand out of my grip. I could tell, even then, what was on his mind at the time. What would a five-year-old know about standards? That was the last time he expressed an opinion on the time it took to get from Kyodo Station to my kindergarten. I placed my Hello Kitty cloth bag on my lap and took out the latest Doraemon comic as the train was just coming to Soshigaya Okura Station.

An accident happened when we were about to leave the train at Kyodo Station. I had quickly grabbed my bag and all of my papers when my book of stickers and my pencil case spilled over my father's knees and onto the floor. I looked toward the doors, where people were crowding so close to each other they looked like a giant sea slug.

"Come along, Emi, or we'll miss our stop," said daddy on his knees, reaching to get one of my pencils that had rolled under a seat. "*Sumimasen* (Excuse me)."

A middle-aged executive, grasping his dark-green leather briefcase against his chest, was lifting his legs high off the floor to allow my father to reach under his seat.

"Don't speak Japanese, daddy! How many times have I told you? It's embarrassing. Now quick, or we really will miss our stop."

The train doors opened and the sea slug of people fell apart on the platform. I stepped off the train and walked ahead. I didn't have to turn around to know that daddy was right behind me.

"Here," he said, "I'm putting these pencils in your red jacket."

"I don't want to wear my jacket now, daddy!"

I knew it was a trick just to get me to wear my jacket.

"I know you don't want to. That's why I'm holding it."

"Daddy, could you build that building? The one they're just putting up. There."

"Daddy's not an architect, Emi, he's a sculptor."

"I know that much, daddy. It's just that I can pronounce architect, but I can't pronounce...the other thing. That's why."

We walked down the shopping street to my kindergarten, a steady stream of people rushing toward us on their way to the station.

"Look, daddy, we're both salmon, you the parent salmon and me the child salmon, going upstream, against the flow of everything. Everything is coming toward us, not stopping, not allowing us for a minute to look to one side or the other or we'll drown. Keep looking ahead, daddy. Are you doing what I say?"

We turned into a narrow lane, and the flow surrounding us stopped. Daddy put my red jacket over my shoulders from behind me.

"There's still a chill in the air. At least wear this until we get to kindergarten."

"But we're almost there. Oh, all right. But it's not for me."

I dashed ahead, with the jacket fluttering like a magician's cape. How much of my life then was I living for my father? There were times when it was necessary to do a thing just to please him, despite the fact that it had nothing in the world to do with me.

I waited by the gate to watch Emi enter the building. The concrete animals in the yard—the little camel, the hippo and the pig—were sitting in their deserted zoo. The surface of the sand in the sandbox had little ridges and crests, just like the sand waves I had once seen with Setsuko in Kyoto at a temple garden.

A gust of wind sent a cloud of cherry blossom petals from the branches overhanging the yard into the sky. They whirled in the air as if in slow motion, finally settling on the sand in the sandbox and the ground of the yard. The little camel, the hippo and the pig were now floating in a pink lake.

Just then the muffle coming from inside the classroom turned into a sharp whine, and through the glass I saw Miss Furui holding a white portable tape recorder with both hands above her head. The song Pata-Pata Mama (Hectic Mama) started to play, and the class went instantly silent. Another gust of wind sent the petals on the ground into a swirl, driving them, a long rolling mound, against the side of the building where they disappeared under the verandah.

At the end of that day I would return to pick Emi up. I would bring her red down jacket for her, though I knew that nothing in the world would make her wear it.

I went on foot from the kindergarten two stations to Soshigaya Okura. People were walking up and down the narrow shopping street, young pregnant women from the enormous apartment block up the road, mothers pushing one baby in a pram with another one strapped to their back, old women and men out for a stroll, children on their way to school loitering in front of the shop that sold Japanese-style wagashi cakes, middle-aged men in suits on bicycles, delivery boys stopping and starting their light trucks, a few farmers pulling carts, and everywhere vertical banners attached to poles fluttering colorful advertisements in the sky, voices calling out, beckoning customers, summoning friends, tinny music filling the air with announcements for products, and amidst it all a single strip of blue sky, following the street all the way up from the station, between the tall poles and wires that lined and crisscrossed it. A beautiful pregnant woman, with a belly like a watermelon and long shiny black hair, was coming straight toward me, beaming.

ON THE NIGHT THAT MY FATHER LET THE BATH WATER overflow, my mother came home much later than normal. I was awakened by the slamming of the front door. I got out of bed and opened my bedroom door just enough to peek through it. It was easy to see that my mother was drunk.

She bent over to take off one shoe but lost her balance, leaning against the wall and knocking our print of Van Gogh's "Starry Night" off its hook. She managed to catch the picture before it hit the floor of the entryway and sat down, putting it to one side. She removed her other shoe. Taking a deep breath with each step, she went to the kitchen and opened the refrigerator. With the refrigerator door half open she turned her head abruptly to my door. But my room was dark and she did not see me. She closed the refrigerator door, sighed twice and went through my father's studio into the bedroom. I followed her.

The studio had a workbench against the wall, and on it were my father's "people," as I called them, tall skinny clay figures in many different poses, eating, drinking, sleeping, reading, swimming, playing tennis, doing it all alone. Nobody was doing anything with anybody else, like talking or dancing. I picked up the statue of a drinking man and I put it beside the one of a reading woman. I placed an eating woman next to a sleeping man. Standing between the workbench and the wall closest to the bedroom I could see my parents' bed through an opening in the door. My mother was looking down on the bed where my father was sleeping on his stomach under a sheet.

Suddenly she grabbed a corner of the sheet and pulled it off him. It floated slowly to the floor like a parachute. My father, who is very tall and whose feet stick out over the edge of the bed, wasn't wearing anything. My mother took off all of her clothes. It was the first time that I had seen either my mummy or daddy naked. Then she climbed on top of my father, onto his back, like someone riding a horse. I covered my mouth and clamped my lips shut. I really had to giggle very badly. After all, now my parents actually did look like a single animal. My mother's long black hair hung down over my father's face.

My father stirred, groaning, then rotated his body toward the middle of the bed, sending my mother rolling over to her own side of the bed. He realized now what my mother had done, but by the time she was on her back with her neck on her pillow, she was asleep and quietly snoring. I knew that my father would look in my direction after that, so I stood as tall as I could with my back against the wall, trying to disappear. I saw his arm stretch out to the floor and pull the sheet back over him and my mother.

I went back to my own room, but not until I had put the statues back in their place, a safe distance from each other.

THE NEXT MORNING I HAD BREAKFAST WITH BOTH MY mother and father. They barely said a word to each other, though they were sitting so close to each other that all they would have to do is stretch out their hand to touch. One of them may as well not have been there. I sometimes think that they are here but at different times, or that the bodies that I see are really photographs taken a long time ago, enlarged and propped up on chairs.

My mother left, saying that she would be home late again. They are apparently renovating one section of a floor of the department store and my mother is in charge of the new boutiques that will occupy the space.

"I'm going now," she said. "Just, Emi, just get some new socks, will you? I noticed that the ones hanging out on the balcony this morning had holes in them. Bye."

My father started to clean up the breakfast dishes. He had made us fried eggs, bacon and toast, coffee for himself and my mother, and a cup of warm Milo for me. I like the way he makes the Milo, mixing in all the powder with hot water before pouring the milk so there aren't any lumps floating on top.

"Daddy, about the socks. I agree with mummy. The problem is that you buy them at Nagasakiya. I mean, I know they're cheap, but socks that are three pairs for a thousand yen just don't last very long. I suggest that you get them in Shinjuku at one of the big department stores like Halc."

"Your mother works at a department store. She could just as easily buy your socks for you."

"Mummy is very busy, daddy, all day long and even at night. She's got a real job. If you had a proper job, daddy, I would say the same thing for you."

"I see," he said, smiling at me and throwing the tea towel

over his left shoulder.

"See what I mean?"

"Being a sculptor was a proper job for Giacometti."

"Yeah, you always tell me about him. But you're not Giacometti, are you, daddy."

"No, that's for sure."

He was putting on a pair of rubber gloves to wash our plates.

"Those rubber gloves are too tight for you, you know."

"Yes, I know. They don't make my size in Japan."

"They would if you went to Shinjuku, to a department store. You never listen, daddy. You just go and do things everything your own way."

"I've got to. No one else does things around here."

I could tell that my father was feeling sorry for himself.

"It's up to you, daddy," I said, pointing my finger directly into his face. "If you want to buy the cheap socks and keep buying them over and over again, you have to expect that people like me and mummy will point that out to you."

There was little I could do to change my father's ways. The most well-intentioned comment was taken by him as wounding. The only thing left for me to do was to tolerate or overlook his faults.

"Are you ready to go to kindergarten?"

"I'm getting ready, can't you see that?"

"Sorry. Don't forget your jacket. It's hanging up."

"You get it for me, daddy. You're the one who thinks I should have it all the time."

"Not all the time. Just until it warms up."

"It is warm now. I don't need it, I tell you, daddy! I just don't need it!"

It's his red jacket, not mine. It's his!

Maybe I was a bit too cruel to my father, even if he wasn't

Giacometti. He did have an exhibition in Kyoto once. But that was before I was born, when my parents were living in Kyoto. I think daddy was happier when he was living in Kyoto.

I WENT INTO MY PARENTS' BEDROOM. I OPENED A DRAWER of my mother's dresser and found one of her brassieres with pretty lace on it. Under the brassiere was a small photo album with a soft felt cover. There were photographs in it that I had never seen before. My parents by a river, in parks, in front of the huge red gate of a shrine, walking at night along a narrow path or alley with lots and lots of restaurants and bars on both sides of it. It is winter, there are little piles of snow along the sides of the path, and in the background I can see a lady in a kimono and high clogs standing by a doorway with her back to the path, and a photograph of my mother and father kissing, with their arms tightly wound around each other, standing on a bridge overlooking a river at night.

I took one of my father's marker pens that he had left on top of the dresser and wrote in English the only words I knew how to write on the back of the photograph of my parents kissing…

Mummy happy   Daddy happy

I slipped the photograph into its plastic pocket, closed the album, placing it carefully under the pretty brassiere again, pushed the drawer in and put the pen back on the dresser.

I went into my father's studio. He wasn't there. He wasn't in the kitchen either. There was only one other place he could be. He had fallen asleep on top of my bed, with his legs dangling loosely from the knees off the edge, like a marionette's. His head was pushed to one side, his arms folded over his chest. He looked really peaceful sleeping there. The last thing I ever wanted to do was to disturb him. So I just climbed over the foot of the bed and lay next to him, face to face. I could feel the breath coming out of his nostrils onto my cheek. I put my right palm against his hip and shut my eyes, and I could see all of his statues in the dark under my eyelids dancing in a big circle, not holding hands, not paying attention to each other, but still dancing together in perfect rhythm with my father's breathing, one step, two steps, round and round as real people not at all as statues, and the people surrounding them, lots of them from the train and the kindergarten with mothers and teachers too, were crowding around the circle trying to get a closer look at the dancers, but those people were made of clay not skin and bones, gray all over, even over their faces, right down to the center of their bodies. This was not at all a bad dream like the one I had when my mother and father rushed in scared to death for me. This was a truly beautiful dream, and it was probably the same dream that my father was having at that very moment. I could tell that much just by looking into his closed eyes.

He wasn't beside me in the morning. But I could feel his breath against my cheek even after he was gone. This was the breath that carried the thoughts and dreams from my daddy directly into me.

SETSUKO USUALLY DOESN'T GO TO THE STORE ON Wednesdays but that week there was a special meeting concerning the remodeling of the seventh floor. We dropped Emi off at the home of a friend, Sakagami Yukiko, a single mother with three small children of her own. Yukiko was to take them all, including Emi, to Tama Zoo.

It happened when I was giving a lecture, which I did

occasionally, at a private art school near Omote Sando Station. The lecture was about Alberto Giacometti. Giacometti's people were scraped and cut, denuded of all outer covering and left to stand by themselves. In an instant, a single soft touch of a hand would send them to the ground to crumble. "Works of art are never finished," he had said.

Mr. Hashizume, head of the school, rushed into the lecture hall. I was standing in the glare of the screen, a picture of one of Giacometti's thin striding figures streaked across my face. Squinting at Mr. Hashizume, the only thing I noticed was his gaping mouth.

"Mister York!" he shouted.

That was all, just my name. Every eye in the lecture hall was on me in the screen.

Sakagami Yukiko had been leading the four children on the pavement alongside a busy street, walking quickly to catch the bus, when her little daughter, Erina, wandered into the street. Emi ran after her. A car with two young men in it could not stop in time. Traffic came to an immediate halt and an ambulance arrived minutes later, but Emi had been instantly killed by the car with the two young men in it.

"I'm what Japanese people call a 'half,' aren't I, daddy?" she had once asked me.

"Yes, you are, petal."

"Which half am I, daddy?"

"Both," I had replied.

On the day of my excursion to Tama Zoo, both my father and mother dressed up, he in his new Issey Miyake reversible coat, with green striped satin on the inside and gray tweed on the outside, and she in her white Jurgen Lehl pants suit that looked like inside-out pajamas. I was being forced to wear a little blue dress that somebody had given me for my fifth birthday.

"It is polite to wear something that you have been given," said my mother. "Sakagami Yukiko gave you this. And now she's taking you to the zoo."

"She gave this dress to me because she's your friend. You never wear that orange sweater that daddy gave you. Besides, her children are revolting. I can't stand them."

"I'm afraid I must agree with Emi on that score," said my father. "They are not very well-behaved children."

"Yukiko has had a very difficult time," said my mother. "Her husband walked out on her and will not pay her any money to look after their children. She gave up a full-time job at Yasuda Life Insurance to get married and now she is only re-hired temporarily to bring in clients for them. They are using her to sell life insurance to all of her friends' husbands and when that supply runs out, they will drop her."

"She tried to sell me a policy, too."

"Why didn't you buy one, daddy? You don't want to leave mummy and me with no money, do you?"

"You can always sell my sculpture after I'm dead. All right, stop laughing. Just kidding."

"No one is interested in buying your statues while you are alive, daddy, so why would anyone want to buy them after you're dead?"

Yukiko lived near Shimokitazawa Station, so it was convenient for both of my parents to deliver me to her house. It was strange traveling on the train with both of them, sitting in between them like I was a clam. People on the train could not help but stare at us. I usually stared right back at them, squinting my eyes at them, but that was only when I was alone with my father. Now I just bowed my head pretending to be shy, clasping my hands together in my lap.

We reached her house after a five-minute walk from the station. It was an old wooden house, with new apartment blocks towering over it on both sides. The path to the front door led through a jungle of overgrown plants. When we came to the door we could hear screaming coming from inside the house. The screaming stopped for a moment, and my mother took the opportunity to slide the front door open and call out.

"Excuse me!"

Yukiko, who was my mother's age but looked much older, came down the stairs in a house dress, holding a one-year-old baby girl in her arms. The baby was crying her eyes out.

"Oh, sorry, I didn't hear you," she said. "Please come in. Hello, Emi."

"Hello."

"What a pretty dress."

"You gave it to me."

"Did I? Oh dear, I am so *occhokochoi* (scatterbrained) these days."

"That means she forgets everything, daddy."

"You needn't translate everything, Emi," said my father, reaching out to take the screaming baby from Yukiko's arms.

"I was only trying to help you!"

I ran upstairs. Fuminori, age five, and his sister Erina, age three, were sitting on the tatami of a six-mat room playing with Lego blocks.

"My brother broke my house," said Erina, suddenly wailing and covering her face in her hands. Fuminori grinned at me, all his little teeth and gums showing.

I went to the window and looked down into the garden. My mother and father were motionless on the path, obviously in the midst of an argument. My mother was pointing with a waving finger up to the window.

"Look, Erina, I made your house again," said Fuminori, pulling his little sister's hands from her face.

"My house," she cried, smiling up at me. "Look, Emi, it's my house."

There seemed to be no air in that room at all, and I felt as if I would die if I didn't take the deepest breaths. We stayed where we were, absolutely still, without saying a single word, for a long time. Even Fuminori and Erina didn't budge, staring at the colorful little house made of blocks. I wish my daddy could have made statues of us then. I only wish he knew how to make a real statue of me.

Setsuko would not remember it, the beautiful women in kimono, their long silk sleeves draping down, dancing with open fans in their hands on covered boats on the river in Kyoto at night, lantern lights radiating reflections that moved over the tops of the shallow waves like fireflies flitting across water. She was off somewhere, I could not reach her, always walking down a blinding bright corridor in her department store with a million consumers on her mind. Never far from there. It was pointless to ask her about memories. I never reminded my wife of things and soon forgot them myself.

I could guess what my parents were arguing about. The new boutiques were about to open for business in her department store. She couldn't say when she'd be home. He might be held up by students after his lecture. But he would come straight here once he could get away. I felt sorry for them bickering like that, but there was very little that I could do about it. I just wanted them to know that I was not the cause of it. Not me. They are the cause of it. They themselves.

My parents suddenly looked up at the second-story window and gave me a very funny look. Normally I would tell them to stop it. But today I felt embarrassed and, I guess, a little sad, so I just smiled down at them.

I said goodbye to my mother from the top of the stairs. In the entryway she waved her hand once in front of her face and walked out the door. My father was handing Yukiko an envelope, which she refused to take but finally did...I think that it had money in it. I came down the stairs and stood in front of him. He knelt down to my level.

"It won't be long now, Emi," he said, kissing me gently on the cheek.

"I know, daddy."

"I love you," he whispered.

He stood up. Daddy looked so very very tall to me then. He was always like a tower, my daddy. He disappeared without sliding the door shut.

The three children were fighting in the upstairs room, crawling over each other, a ball with twelve limbs squirming like worms around it.

"Fuminori," I said. "Stop it please. Come on, I have something secret to tell you."

The limbs froze, retracting, the bodies disentangled and in an instant the three children were sitting crosslegged on the tatami in front of me.

"What is it, Emi?" asked Fuminori.

"What is it? What is it?" repeated Erina. Even the baby seemed to be saying this to me with her tiny eyes.

"Well," I had to make this up as I spoke, "well, you see, you know that panda that has just come to Japan."

"Panda, panda!" cried Fuminori.

"Panda, panda!" repeated Erina.

"Pa-n-da," said the baby softly, gurgling.

"Listen, she spoke," said Fuminori. "The baby said her very first word!"

"No," said his little sister. "She already said 'mama.'"

"That's not a word."

"Yes it is. It is a word too!"

"Shhh. Anyway, listen, it is just possible that the panda will be at our zoo today." I knew that it wouldn't.

"Really?" said the two of them in unison.

"Well, it is possible, you know. Let's hold hands and walk together all the way down the stairs and on the street and see what happens. All right?"

Fuminori, Erina and I went down the stairs carefully together. I was holding the baby close to my chest.

It was late morning and my mother would already have been at her department store by now. I can see her smiling broadly, bowing to a crowd of customers in front of one of the new boutiques, her boss right beside her. He is a handsome and tall Japanese man with streaks of gray hair at his temples, wearing a glossy green silk tie and absolutely stinking of aftershave lotion like all those men in Japanese elevators do. He says to her, "Setsuko-san, good work. Well done. Congratulations. You deserve a lot of credit." But my mother is always properly modest when at work. "Oh no, Mr., uh, Suzuki..." (The "uh" is mine because I don't know if his name is really Suzuki or something else) ... She'll say, "I have done nothing out of the ordinary. The team deserves the credit, not me. Everyone has been so marvelous." And the hundreds of excited housewives, their luxury handbags bulging, money dripping out of them like food out of a baby's mouth, nearly stampede to get their hands on the goods before anyone else does. They know that it's not what you buy, as my mother says, but whether you have it before others do that counts. And I can see my daddy too. He is standing perfectly erect in his classroom with all eyes on him. The people in that classroom worship him. After all, he has changed their lives. Before they met him they had a drab, really uninteresting life with no surprises and nothing to bring light into their lives. But now my daddy is telling them these amazing things about people who have been captured in a moment by Alberto Giacometti, petrified real live statues stopped in their tracks! The slide of one of the statues is being projected on a screen right now and my daddy is standing in the light, blocking it, his face half covered by the picture. He is in the picture himself and the people are looking up at him. His face lit up. Then, all of sudden there is another man in the room. It is the principal of the school, Mr. Hashizume, and he is flinging the door open, panting, desperately gasping for breath. All of the people snap their heads to him, away from my father and his picture, and he says, almost in a scream, "Mr. York!"

"Hold hands!" I screamed to Fuminori.

His mother was holding the baby against her chest, as little Erina grasped onto her skirt. The bus was just pulling in and a man brushed against me, running to catch it. Erina's hand had just slipped off her mother's skirt, but her mother hadn't noticed. She was gripping the baby tightly, about to step up onto the bus.

Just then little Erina stepped off the curb and began, for no reason on earth, to cross the street in front of the bus. The bus had come to a standstill and Erina's mother had climbed onto it, thinking that Erina was still clutching her skirt.

"Do not move!" I ordered Fuminori in the angriest tone of voice that I have ever spoken with in my life. I ran after Erina, who was now even with the right headlight of the bus. One or two more steps would take her into the very middle of the street where a stream of cars was overtaking the bus. I jumped into the street in front of the stopped bus, reaching out for her shoulder. But I could not catch hold of her dress, missing it by the length of a baby finger. I remember the dress's color very well. It was all white. She had a little shiny black leather belt around her waist. I ran around her and stood in front of her. This stopped her in her tracks.

"Get back!" I shouted to her.

The bus driver had been leaning forward and saw everything that was happening in front of his bus.

Erina turned around, just like a tiny ballet dancer in a music box, and the expression on the face of the bus driver turned from a smile into something awful. His mouth that had been a line was now a gaping black hole, and his eyes, his eyes were open into deep hollow pits, and his hair was standing on end like shiny needles, long sharpened needles that can't be bent.

I had only a split second to see the front of the car that was accelerating alongside the bus. The passenger was a young man, at least three times my age. I think he saw me before the driver did. The driver of the car had his head down. He seemed to be reaching for something that had fallen down. All I could see was the black hair on the top of his head. Suddenly he raised his head, and I saw that he had wrap-around sunglasses on. He was smoking a cigarette. Those were the last things that I could take note of.

The front bumper of the car collided with my stomach, and I must have slumped forward, because before I was knocked back I felt the hot grill of the car hit my face. The back of my skull smashed into the street and I heard a very loud CRACK! I don't know why, but I rolled over onto my stomach against the curb as the left front tire drove over my back. My entire body was crushed by this. The bones in my back and my ribs were not so hard, seeing as I was only five years old, and my thin body was now flat, without dimension.

ONE YEAR LATER

EVERY YEAR WITHOUT FAIL, AFTER COMING TO LIVE IN TOKYO, Nick and Setsuko had taken Emi, first on their back and later in her Aprica pram, to Yoyogi Park to view the giant forsythia bush in bloom, and then, with early summer, to Kamakura for the flowering hydrangea. These have no blossoms this year, thought Nick, the buds did not form or having formed would not flower, or having flowered, did so in a uniform gray. And the sky displayed the texture of coarse cloth, only intensifying the drabness of everything below it. Not worth going. Not worth looking at. Forget it.

Nick was walking on the narrow path between grassed areas at Yoyogi Park. He had taken the local train from Seijo Gakuenmae, changing to the Chiyoda Line at Yoyogi Uehara, getting off at Yoyogi Koen Station. It was morning and the train had been filled with school children carrying heavy dark-red backpacks, some of them in their first year of primary school, milling silently together, gaping at each other with eyes full of trepidation and wonder. Will not look at them. Won't allow myself to look at these children. He moved through the cars of the train to the very front, then stood with his back to everyone, staring along the rails, closing his eyes when entering a station as he did while passing in a car by cemeteries at country churches as a child. I remember racing around one at Glendalough, he thought, smoothed-down graves, on some of them a tiny skull and crossbones carved in relief for the dead children, my hand running along the iron bars of the fence around it. And when I came to the last bar, back at the entrance, I gripped it so tightly, knowing that I had gone around once. Then I could open my eyes and breathe.

On the train at Shimokitazawa he had recognized one of the kindergarten mothers. It was late morning. Nick purposely avoided early trains. Not willing to meet up with someone taking her child there, can't do that. Now, by chance, this mother had come through the door at the very front of the train. Bloody hell! God...God dammit! Their glances met but instantly swerved to the side and down. Will not recognize that glance, he thought, will not give in to hideous coincidence. It did not happen, that's all there is to it. Nick turned his back to her and returned his stare to the rails.

At Yoyogi Uehara he had nearly fallen out of the train car, stumbling over his foot, his arms thrust out at right angles to his body in anticipation of a fall, his torso bent ahead of him on legs that felt like sticks, then finally into the men's toilet where he retched nothing more than gas from his mouth.

"Tomorrow is the first anniversary of Emi's death," Setsuko had told him the night before, standing behind him in his studio with her palms resting on his shoulders. "We will have to get through that as best as we can. Perhaps, I mean, well, Nick, just perhaps you could think of teaching at the art school or something. Mr. Hashizume did once say that you would be welcome at any time. It would only be parttime, and you could still do your sculpture."

Nick had not answered her, continuing to carve the thinnest slivers of hardened clay off a statue of an archer. He picked up the archer and examined it, but suddenly the clay string on the bow snapped.

"I'm sorry. I shouldn't try to talk to you when you're working."

Setsuko went to the kitchen and sat at the table, leaning her head heavily in her hand, half slumped over.

There were few people out on this drizzly July day as Nick

marched along the paths, crisscrossing the park. He noticed that he was being followed by two high school students, one of them with a tape recorder strapped over his shoulder.

"Hello, excuse me," called one of them. "Hello, excuse me, sir!"

The student with the tape recorder bolted ahead, tapping him on the arm.

"Please, sir, may we do interview of you? It is for school," he said in halting English.

"Not now," said Nick, abruptly turning off the path and jogging over the grass.

I am not going to stop moving, he thought, not for anyone or anything. No matter what events occur in front of me I will disregard them. I may be forced to witness them, but I will not take them in. Nothing will get to me, not today or any day. He went ahead like that, crisscrossing the park again and again, winding through it as if proceeding on a track dug into the soil, as if his right leg was constantly ahead of his left on the moving track and he needed nothing more to go forward than to will it, motion in a state of utter stillness.

He returned home in the afternoon to find Sakagami Yukiko, Fuminori and Erina in the four-and-a-half-mat tatami room, kneeling in front of Emi's altar, with the baby, now two years old, standing beside them. On the altar were Emi's stuffed parrot, her Hello Kitty bag, the Doraemon comic books that she had been reading at the time of her accident and a framed photograph of her standing among the concrete camel, hippopotamus and pig in the kindergarten yard.

Yukiko and her two elder children immediately sat up straight, lowering their heads to the floor in a bow. Even the two-year-old bowed, wobbling back and forth on her feet before falling forward.

"Stand up!" said her mother angrily, straightening her into a standing position again. "I'm sorry."

"No, please," said Nick. "No need to do that. Please just go on as before. Can I get you some tea or something?"

Nick now noticed Setsuko kneeling stiffly in the corner of the room, a handkerchief clutched in her hand. She peered at him, trying to form a smile with her tightly closed lips.

"I'll get some tea," said Nick, leaving the room.

Fuminori, in a tight-fitting black suit and black necktie, crawled on his knees to Setsuko in the corner of the room, bowed his head deeply once then raised it and, tightening the knot of his necktie, said, "We have nothing at all that we can say to you." He looked back at his mother, who nodded her head for him to continue. "We have, uh, nothing we, so, please forgive my mother, me and my two little sisters. Please." He once again looked to his mother, whose cheeks were running with tears.

Setsuko, still on her knees, bowed to the four of them, keeping her head down for seconds. When she raised it, the two-year-old girl was standing directly in front of her. She stretched out her hand to touch Setsuko's hair. Setsuko gently took hold of the hand, brought it toward her and put it to her cheek.

"Thank you for coming," she said. "Thank all of you for coming today."

Some moments later Nick heard Yukiko say "*Gomen kudasai* (goodbye)" from the entryway, the front door opened and closed, and the apartment was silent again.

He observed the steam rising from his cup of green tea, a wisp of smoke that broke into two streams then three, then fragmented in the air. He looked up at the kitchen ceiling, fixing his gaze on the flickering fluorescent light. There were ways to get through this day. There is no reason why this day should be any more unbearable than any other, no reason on earth. Setsuko, still kneeling in the corner of the tatami room with the altar, might speak to me, he thought, but her words will not affect me, not touch me. I will hear them and I may answer them, but they will make no difference to me, not to me.

The two of them sat like that for some time, she on her knees in the corner of the tatami room with the altar, and he at the kitchen table over an untouched cup of green tea until long after the incense placed by Yukiko and her three children in the little brass sand pot on Emi's altar had burnt out. As for Emi's room, it had been left as is the last time she was in it. Neither Nick nor Setsuko had set foot in it for nearly a year.

After dark Setsuko finally stood up, her legs aching, and went to Emi's room, stopping at the threshold. Nick, hearing the swishing of her black satin dress, said in a soft quiet voice, without so much as turning his head in her direction, without the least suggestion of bitterness or antagonism, "Leave it. Just leave it be."

Setsuko immediately stepped back and turned away from the room. But she did not respond to him. She went to bed in her black satin dress without eating or drinking and soon fell into a deep sleep.

Nick sat down at his workbench, making a pencil sketch of a tall man standing by a tree. But it was not a tree in Yoyogi Park, not a likeness of himself and not a picture meant to depict his feelings that day.

"This looks like nothing," he whispered to himself, ripping the sketch to shreds and letting the pieces drop onto his lap. I am not going on with this. These statues are worthless.

But he did not destroy them. There is no meaning in that

either, he thought, leave them. Leave everything. There was meaning in leaving things be. In fact, yeah, sure, it's the only bloody thing that does have a meaning. There is no need to obliterate a sky that had already been blotted and drained of all color, no need to look up at a sky that is a sheet of dense cloth descended over everything and everybody, a gray, all-purpose pall, a most convenient fabric. Yes! Every single observation, experience, sight, the slightest noise, the barest whiff of a familiar scent, the gentlest touch, all these need not be given a shape, they need not be reformed into something else, no clay or paper or ink or pencil lead or paintbrush or canvas or color will play the least part in my life.

Nick could breathe freely now, relieved to have overcome his need to create.

SETSUKO WAS SPENDING THE EVENING AS SHE SPENT MOST evenings, drinking in the company of her coworkers at the department store, all of them male, tonight sitting on a high stool at the counter of Bateren, a cozy restaurant in Iidabashi that specialized in fresh shellfish and sake from Kyushu.

"Well, Setsuko-san," said the section chief, Mr. Saito, raising his sake cup, "you have done a stupendous job in customer relations, and thank you all for inviting me tonight. I know that the purpose of these evenings for you is to be able to roast the section chief, namely yours truly, over the coals. Well, tonight, we're roasting all of this lovely fish over the coals instead. Thank you for a job well done. We are now more than halfway through 1987, and all I can..."

"1988, section chief," said Watabe, the youngest of the group. "This year is 1988."

"Oh, I must have had more to drink than I, well, okay then, let it be 1988, even better, and, well, um, so, the Japanese economy is stronger than ever, we have almost no crime, the highest level of education in the world, no major social problems to speak of, the yen is the strongest currency anywhere in the world and, well, um, our department store sales have nowhere to go but up, up and further up."

He drank down the sake that remained in his cup, Watabe deftly refilling it before it was placed back on the counter.

"We should never be complacent, however," said Arai, a man of Mr. Saito's age who had nevertheless been passed over for promotion on several occasions in the past. "No one knows what will happen next year, let alone in the 1990s."

"We will be all right," said the section chief, banging his fist on the counter much more forcefully than he had intended. "Um, we just have to continue doing what we have always been doing. Nothing is going to change, I can tell you that. *Zenshin suru nomi* (Just forge ahead)."

They were all standing outside the restaurant. It was a stifling and oppressive August evening, a moist heavy curtain drawn over the city. The group parted, wishing each other a pleasant Obon holiday. Several of the men, at Watabe's insistence, lured the section chief out for a *nijikai* (further drinks), hopping into a taxi and speeding off in the direction of Akasaka. Setsuko headed with Arai toward Iidabashi Station.

"This must have been a very trying, I mean, an awful year for you," he said, after a long silence.

"Oh, I..." she sighed, running her fingers through the hair by her right ear.

Once again they walked in silence.

"May I offer you a cup of coffee or...?" he asked.

Now she looked into his eyes for the first time since leaving the restaurant. Arai was in his late forties, with a slightly receding but nonetheless full head of black hair, a stylish silver-gray suit, a yellow knit tie and Italian shoes. Why would he ask me, a married woman and a coworker, to have coffee with him, she thought. I have let my hair grow almost to my shoulders, have bought no new clothes for a year and have nothing particularly interesting to say on any subject except how to stimulate consumer demand.

"It's all right," he said. "Of course, it is late and..."

"I would have a beer, if you..."

"A beer? Why, yes. It is so hot. I don't remember Tokyo being this unbearable."

"Oh, it is every year."

They sat by the bay window of a cafe bar near Iidabashi Station as he spoke continually of his family, two boys, one studying chemistry at Tokyo Institute of Technology, the other recently graduated from Hitotsubashi University, now working for Nintendo, showing her photographs from his wallet of the boys when they were in middle school, telling her that he had wanted to be a school teacher himself but had gone into retailing instead, how he had not participated in the student movement in the 1960s but had secretly admired his friends who did.

"And your wife? Does she work as well?" asked Setsuko, finishing her second beer.

"Let me light that for you," he said, pulling a small red disposable lighter from his jacket pocket.

"Thank you," she said, taking a deep drag on her cigarette. "But I thought that you didn't smoke."

"I don't. But I keep this lighter to accommodate our customers. Also, if they offer me a cigarette, of course I can't refuse."

Setsuko looked around the room. A middle-aged couple

were holding hands over a table in the corner, conversing in whispers.

"You asked about my wife."

"Oh yes, sorry. Is she in Tokyo? Of course she's in Tokyo. Sorry, I don't know what I'm asking anymore. I think I have overdone it on the alcohol tonight."

"No, that's fine. She died five years ago."

"Oh, I am sorry."

"No. Breast cancer. She had just turned forty and had always been in the peak of health. Her best friend went to the doctor for a checkup and she decided to go along for a lark."

"For a lark."

"Well, yes, I mean, just to keep her company, really. She consented to have a checkup, a mammogram, herself and they found a cluster of little tumors. They operated immediately but the cancer had already spread into her lymph nodes. She died six months later. I had spent all of my time at the department store, but we were planning an early retirement for me and, once we had the boys out of our way, we were going to live in Europe, you know. She spoke Spanish and Italian, was crazy about Renaissance art and music and, oh dear, I had better put these photographs away. The boys would kill me if they knew I was showing them to people."

The next thing Setsuko heard was him speaking to the manager of the cafe.

"No, she's all right. She just had a bit too much to drink."

"Are you sure?" said the manager. "We can order a taxi for you and your wife, if you wish."

"No, really, see? She's coming to already."

Setsuko had passed out in her chair. She gradually raised her head and looked around. Where is that couple, she thought, they were right there, holding hands, whispering, telling each other little secrets about themselves, what they wish to hear, in what position they prefer to sleep at night, where they like to be touched.... Why aren't they still there? That's all she could think about.

"Where are the others?" she said.

"What others? Oh, they went on to a *nijikai* for more drinks. Are you all right, Setsuko-san?"

"Yes. No, I didn't mean them. Oh God, I shouldn't have had those beers."

"I'm sorry. It's my fault. Now, please let me call you a taxi."

"Oh no. It's too far."

"I insist. Look, I've got a company taxi voucher, still unused. Look, take this. Just sign your name and the amount on it."

The manager of the cafe pulled the chair away as Setsuko stood.

"No, really, I am fine," she said, smiling to both of them. "Thank you. I'm sorry to have caused you worry."

They stood on the curb. Arai hailed a taxi.

"Thank you for tonight," she said, momentarily leaning against him. "You have been very kind to me. Oh dear, I think I'm still tipsy."

A taxi screeched to a stop in front of them. He grabbed her elbow as she stepped off the curb, her knees shaky. Her shoulder bag slipped slowly down her arm.

"Are you sure you...?"

"Yes, I am fine. You have been very kind to me," she said, plopping down in the back of the taxi, telling the driver her address as the upper half of her body lost all strength and she fell easily onto the seat.

Arai Toshiyuki remained on the curb until her taxi was out of sight.

SETSUKO MANAGED TO LEAVE THE DEPARTMENT STORE AT six-thirty. She went down the stairs at Shinjuku 3-Chome Station and along the underground walkway to her Odakyu Line train, which she boarded, pushed along in the middle of a crush of people. It was an unbearably hot and humid early September day, with not the slightest movement of air, with no relief for the skin. Setsuko, unused to commuting at the peaks of the rush hours, was stifled by the closeness. Couldn't go home every day this early, she thought, can't have my back shoved against other people, can't be pressed on all sides, straightened into a stick.

The air conditioner in the car blew warmish air over her hair and finally, at Seijo Gakuenmae Station, she tumbled out, crouching for a moment at the top of the stairs, gasping for a breath. Why am I doing this, she thought, why am I going home early? A woman must be with her loved ones, her husband. Loved? There is no space for that any more. Each day is destined to be a chore, that is the way days are constituted, measured turns of obligation one after the other, time revolving regularly around time and nothing more. Strangers called customers, husbands called loved ones, acquaintances called friends, all begging for attention or devotion, unlike a crowd in a train on an unbearable September evening that only requires you to take up a space and nothing more.

"Are you all right?" asked a girl in a middle-school uniform, crouching beside Setsuko. "There's a police box at the bottom of the stairs."

"Leave me be, I'm fine," said Setsuko, burying her face in her right hand and, with the flick of the wrist of her left, gesturing to the girl to step away.

"I'm sorry," said the girl, descending the stairs and disappearing from view.

Setsuko gradually stood, ironed the front of her skirt with her palm, unbuttoned the top button of her blouse and wiped the nape of her neck with a handkerchief. Two trains that had been traveling in opposite directions stopped at the station and a great throng of people alighted from both of them, the throng marching patiently, as if ordered to do so, toward Setsuko, who was now standing at the very top of the stairs. The throng split in two just before reaching her, sliding easily around her, not paying the least attention to her, taking her into account solely as an unmoving object in its way. What if I was not here? she thought. The only difference would be the absence of an obstacle, an impediment to the straight motion of others. Setsuko took a step forward, cleaving the throng further but making no difference to the flow. Turn around, Setsuko, for God's sake turn around! What will you see, the backs of people, their heads, their bodies? Will you see yourself joining them, a part of them, whisked along, carried in their direction? They will have pulled together, closed the space immediately after slipping by you. What do you expect to see when you look at them, eh? Why would you so much as assume that even one of them would be throwing a casual glance back at you? Who was there at the top of the stairs at that moment? Don't ask me. How should I know? No one was there, for all I know. No one that a single person who passed would recognize or recall. You don't expect the girl in the school uniform to be waiting at the bottom of the stairs looking up at you, do you, worrying about you, wondering what could be the matter with you, why you were crouching with your forearm against the wall, shivering, weeping until you were choking on your tears? Who is she to you? Who do you think you are, Setsuko York, wife and mother of a dead child, who in the hell do you think you are?! Can you be certain that there were no women like you in that stream of others marching toward you, brushing past you as if you were nothing more than a featureless pole in the ground, avoiding you like the plague, the plague of mothers with dead children? Do you think that they will never find themselves as you have now, at the top of a set of stairs or in the middle of the path or alone in their own bedroom, asking themselves what you are asking yourself, wondering if there is a life beyond this, one that at the same time can be solitary and shared, frantic and serene, equally selfish and selfless? Could they be doing what you are doing, allowing themselves a moment to stop and listen to an insistent painful voice inside them that sounds exactly like yours? This is my voice speaking, she thought, it shuts out all other sound, it deafens me to the voices of others. How can I ever know what anyone else has been through? I can't. I won't.

Setsuko was stopped dead until the throng had passed her by, until she was absolutely alone. "Statue of Woman at the Top of Stairs." But something still in me gives me the impetus to take a step down the stairs, and then another, to go home, she thought, or at least to a place called it.

WHAT IS NICHOLAS YORK DOING IN JAPAN? EIGHTH SON OF a butcher from Mort St., downtown Dublin, "fitting name of a street for a profession like mine," father had said. About the only thing my old man ever did say to me. There had to be more to the story than the pat explanation of how he came to leave home, offered to Japanese and non-Japanese alike, that "one day the front door was left open and I just walked out of it, and no one seemed to notice the difference." That may explain how I left Dublin, he thought, but not how I ended up in Japan. The "more to the story" was Yumi, a student of early Irish poetry at Trinity College. Jesus, never thought I'd have a girl friend who spoke Gaelic, let alone a Japanese one. She was the first love, and I thought I would never be able to rid my mind of the picture of her standing above me, naked, gazing down on my bushy blond hair with a smile on her lips, her hands on the sides of my head, lifting it up, gently letting it down, my hands resting on her hips and after it is over for her she says "I feel it in the deep heart's core" and I think to myself, never thought I'd hear a Japanese girl quote Yeats back to me and at such an ironical moment to boot, and from then on for any number of years the words "lapping" and "shore" could not pass me by without my recalling her standing above me with her hands on the sides of my head. I followed her back to Japan, to Kyoto, where she worked on her doctorate at Kyoto University and I enrolled in the sculpture course at Bidai (Kyoto University of Art) where I was taught by Prof. Shiomi Tokunosuke. We lived together in an apartment in Izumikawa-cho in Shimogamo and spoke once or twice of marriage until Yumi fell in love with a divorced American scholar from Yale University who was on sabbatical leave in Kyoto researching descriptions of the incidence of incense clocks in medieval Japanese poetry. Yumi discontinued work on her doctorate and left Japan for New Haven, Connecticut, in the company of Assistant Professor Richard Levitt, becoming Mrs. Richard Levitt the following year, 1979, and sending me a postcard half in English and half in Gaelic from her honeymoon with her new husband and his nine-year-old son, Evan, from Greece, depicting a bust of Byron with the words written, in her hand, across it, "I think, therefore iamb." Shortly after that I met Setsuko at a party for foreigners and English-speaking Japanese in Yoshidayama, we started seeing each other, taking long walks up and down the Kamo River, soon began living together in an old rented

Japanese-style house at Shobuen-cho in Kamigamo, and, in November 1979, were married at the Kitaku Ward Office. Her parents came down to Kyoto from Tokyo, hosting a reception for us at the Miyako Hotel.

I didn't notify my parents of the wedding until after Emi's birth in 1982, and my mother wrote back to say that dad had passed away and that she was very happy for me and wished all well, but "since I never would be able to speak Japanese it makes no sense really for me ever to meet Emi, does it, if we've nothing to say to each other." That was the last communication that I had with anyone in my family back home, except for intermittent letters from my little brother, Jack.

Thanks to Prof. Shiomi's generous praise of my sculpture, I began to receive a degree of recognition in Kyoto, holding my first one-man show at the Iteza Gallery on Sanjo-dori, with nearly all of the pieces purchased by a wealthy Osaka collector named Tani. Winning the 1982 Kyoto Novice's Art Prize led to an exhibit at Takashimaya Department Store in Osaka, though the works for that show, coinciding with the Emi's birth, were nothing like what I was to do later. I carved realistic humans then, scaling them down until they were half their normal size. No works from the Takashimaya show sold, though Takahashi Keiji, eminent art critic, made the trip down from Tokyo to review it in *Geijutsu Shincho*. Prof. Shiomi ripped up the issue of the magazine with that review in front of a class of students, remarking, in English, "I wouldn't even wipe my ass with this." His final piece of advice to me was, "Do not fear to change your direction at any time in your career. The statues that you make of people are statues of aspects of your own personality. Not to change them is the same as not recognizing the growth in your own spirit."

We are here, thought Nick in the blissful months after Emi's birth, the three together in Kyoto, going everywhere together, doing everything together, finding unending joy in each other. I am here in Japan because here I am free from the dreary and painful ties of home, here I can sever myself from my past and truly leave it behind me. Here I can become the man I wish to be, only here with Setsuko and now with Setsuko and Emi together.

WHEN THEIR SON WAS STILLBORN A YEAR AFTER Emi's birth, Setsuko had stayed in hospital for three weeks, recovering. Nick could not continue sculpting for six months, the very existence of the statues in their immobile state bringing back the baby lying on the birthing table after the umbilical cord had been cut and Setsuko had been led away. Nick was called into the room by the obstetrician at Kyoto Prefectural University of Medicine Hospital, Dr. Harada, who said, holding Nick's arm, "There was nothing that we could have done. At any rate, it would have been deformed, Mr. York, and not lived long. It is better this way. As for the future, I advise your wife not to have any more children. This has been a great shock for her. She bled a great deal. All of the details will be in the *boshi techo*, the mother-child record book. I'm afraid that even babies who are stillborn must have such a record book. It is a Japanese custom. I am sorry, Mr. York."

Nick went to Setsuko and attempted in vain to comfort her, but she was beside herself with grief and had to be heavily sedated. He left the hospital, picked up Emi, who was being looked after by an Australian couple, the McNaughtons, both ceramic artists, childless, living for over twenty years in a dilapidated traditional house on Teramachi-dori north of Marutamachi-dori, and pushed her in her pram through the streets, revisiting the sites that he had been to with Setsuko before they were married, talking to Emi all the while about the past, the view, the trees and flowers, the light, the air. "This is where mummy and daddy fell in love, Emi. Right here, not so long ago, before you were born, mummy and daddy," he said, taking her to the exact spots, with her in place of Setsuko.

WHAT DO I HAVE TO FEAR FROM RECOLLECTION, he wondered. Was I so happy before and am I so miserable now that my mind will not tolerate even a moment's contemplation? The answer is that there is no further need to contemplate, each day flows from the one before without plan, without the need for calculation. I am being propelled through that, instinct alone the engine of desire. That previous man was not me, it was someone else, some other Nicholas York in my guise. Let him live and die, what do I care?

Only when Nick walked was he able to entirely blot from his mind the rushing memories of the person he once was.

It was while he was on the edge of the moat by the entrance to the Fairmont Hotel, drawn there because he and Setsuko had spent nights in the hotel on a trip to Tokyo when she was pregnant with Emi, that a Japanese woman, twenty-five years old, sat down on his bench. She watched him dozing, his long legs stretched out, his back as straight as a stick, his arms folded over his belly, his chin on his chest. What country was he from? she wondered. Probably America, or England. Married to a Japanese? She noticed the ring before anything else. An English teacher, no doubt, about, well, five years in Japan. He began to mumble in his sleep but the words, distinctly English, were unintelligible. A good way to polish my English, she thought, listening to a native speaker talk through his dreams.

Normally she would have left before this tall foreign man awakened. If she didn't, they would have to say a word to each other, at least acknowledge each other's presence. Avoid that embarrassment, she thought. But something was restraining her on the bench, she felt that she could not move from there, that she needed to see herself there in the shadow of the long row of the moat's cherry blossom trees congested with dark-green leaves, that somehow she was obliged to watch over this man, if only until he stirred and spoke a clear word.

"Oh dear," said Nick, snapping out of his sleep and seeing the young woman at the other edge of the bench. He sat immediately upright and cleared his throat.

"Please excuse me if I disturbed you," she said in English.

"Oh, no problem. Sorry, I must've dozed off."

The two were silent. Both felt the urge to stand and walk away in opposite directions at exactly the same moment, but neither moved.

"I, uh, didn't mean to disturb you."

"You speak excellent English."

"Oh, thank you. I have studied at university in Great Britain."

"Oh really? Where?"

"Durham."

"Know it well."

"Oh, so you are English."

"No, Irish. Sorry."

"No, I am sorry. I was wondering when you were asleep. We say, *shirakawa yofune*. You were on a nighttime boat on the Shirakawa River. It means, dead in the world."

"Dead to the world. Yep, that's me, all right."

"Oh well, I didn't mean it that way."

"No, lovely expression," he said. "Is that the Shirakawa

River in Kyoto?"

"Oh my goodness, you know so well. I think you speak Japanese fluently."

"No, actually, very poorly. But I have lived in Kyoto."

"Oh, that is where I am from!"

Nick now looked at her closely for the first time. She was fixing her gaze on the moat, where a swan swam in a circle by the castle wall's edge. A very pretty girl, he thought. In the old days I'd think it fate meeting someone like this on a bench. Slightly on the plump side, with a more pronounced figure than most Japanese women have, salmon-colored skin and short cropped hair, her light-brown skirt riding up above her knees. Don't ask her name, just say thank you, goodbye and walk away.

"I can't believe you know Kyoto," she said, interrupting his train of thought.

"So, uh, where in Kyoto are you from then?"

"Me? Well, do you know Nakagyoku?"

"You mean in the center of town?"

"Yes, that's it. Well, my father sold furniture on Ebisugawa-dori."

"Know it well."

"You do? That's amazing. I went to the local school, then on to Ritsumeikan University and..."

"When was that? Perhaps we were at university at the same time."

"Oh, did you go to Ritsumei, too?"

"No. I was at Bidai."

"Oh, you are an artist," she said, turning toward him.

"Well, of sorts. I mean, I was. Haven't done much lately. So, uh, how did you get over to England?"

"A scholarship. I was doing a master's degree on Lafcadio

Hearn."

"Ah, another Irishman."

"Oh yes. Do you like him?"

"Not really. Never had much time for that old exotic stuff."

"Oh yes, you are right. But he was a fascinating man. Do you know he is buried in Tokyo?"

"No, I didn't."

"Yes, at Zoshigaya Cemetery."

"Zoshigaya. That's near where I live, in Seijo. I never knew there was a cemetery there."

"Oh, I think you mean *So*-shigaya. That's different. This is *Zo*-shigaya."

"Oh, sorry. You see, never did learn Japanese properly. No better at French either, really."

"That does not matter. Perhaps we can go one day to Zoshigaya Cemetery. I will show you where his body is buried. There are many other famous Japanese in their graves there too, Izumi Kyoka, Natsume Soseki, you know him? Nagai Kafu, Kindaichi Kyosuke."

"I'm afraid I'm not much of a literary person. But I do know Natsume Soseki. Didn't he write a book about the snow country?"

"No, that was Kawabata Yasunari."

"Oh. You see, literature's really not my thing."

"But you know so much about art!" she said out of the blue, with an unexpected enthusiasm.

Their eyes met, then Nick's gaze followed her body down from her open neck over her breasts to her hips and finally her exposed thighs. She sat forward again, pulling the hem of her skirt toward her knees.

"I am Yuko Maeno. And how shall I call you?"

"You can call me Nick. Nick York."

She thrust her hand out and they shook, then, taking a mechanical pencil and her pocket diary from her handbag, wrote YUKO and, beside it, her telephone number, ripped out the page and handed it to him.

"Call me and we'll go to see Lafcadio Hearn's body," she said, standing. She walked along the moat in the direction of Kudanshita, glancing back once to throw a big smile at him.

Nick put the piece of paper in his pocket, stretched out his legs again and, with the image of a covered boat floating along a river at night in his mind's eye, was soon fast asleep.

TWO PEOPLE DO NOT COMMUNICATE WHEN ONE IS desperate not to. I am braving this dinner, thought Nick, as he and Setsuko went through their courses at Pomme de Terre. I will be attentive to the woman in front of me, acknowledging her little polite gestures and acting on her mild complaints. But nothing will affect me, because the present is just a thing to get through, nothing more than a transition to more of the same.

"Nice sardines" was his sole comment during the entrée, "ravioli's a bit bland" for the main course. Yet Setsuko, for her part, would not give in. She persisted with a patter on every minute aspect of her daily life.

"Really, that's grand," said Nick in a monotone, stirring a teaspoon of sugar into his coffee.

"Is that all you can say? This is my life, Nick. It's our life."

"Is it? How so?"

"What do you say that for? You really have turned into a man with no heart. What are you made of?"

Setsuko gripped the cloth napkin in her lap. She fought back tears and clenched her teeth. But she wouldn't take her eyes off of him.

"Made of stone. Or didn't you know it when you married me. You want another dessert?"

"No."

"Then let's go."

Nick rose, waving a hand to the waiter.

"How did you enjoy the meal?" asked the waiter, a young man with a mustache, handing Nick the bill.

"Very nice," he replied.

"*Arigato gozaimashita* (Thank you very much)," said the waiter, followed by shouts of these two words from behind the counter and the kitchen.

The two stood outside the restaurant. It was raining steadily, the first October chill in the air. Setsuko pulled the front of her cardigan closed and folded her arms over her chest. Nick held an umbrella over himself and her.

"Nick," she finally said, putting her hand on his waist and grasping his belt tightly with her index finger and thumb. "How long are we going to go on like this?"

"Like what?"

"Like this. Being with each other and being totally apart at the same time. It's hell, Nick. I can't take it much longer. I've got this and a very hectic job and..."

"Yes, I know how busy you are at your job. You've always been busy at the job, while I sit at home and do fuck all, is that what..."

"No, I never think that. I never meant it that way. You are an artist, darling, and you have to be at home and have all the time in the world on your hands, otherwise you would..."

"So I have all the time in the world, do I now?" he said, angrily. "To do what? You tell me. When did I last create something, produce something? That's what you're trying to say, isn't it."

"No, not at all."

She pulled her hand back and held onto the umbrella handle just below his hand.

"Then what, eh?" said Nick. "You talk and talk and talk and, believe me, I do listen to you, but there's nothing in it. You're really talking for your own sake, to get it out or something, I don't know."

He looked down the street. An old woman, hunched over, was dragging an empty supermarket trolley through the rain. She passed them and turned the corner in the direction of the Odakyu Line tracks as bells sounded, signaling the lowering of the booms, and stopping all traffic.

"Listen, please just listen to me now," she said, pushing her body against his. "I love you, Nick. I have really thought about this a long time. I mean, what is my life? Why should I be punished for going on after Emi's death? I kept my job and I try to do it like before." She paused for a moment, choking, about to sob, then took two deep breaths and continued. "You are not the only one who suffers, Nick. I know how you feel. I really do. But what do you expect me to do about it? We lost our child. Both of us."

"Nothing."

The signal bells went silent and Nick looked for the old woman with her empty trolley.

"Look, let's go," he said.

"Not yet," she said, gripping the front of his shirt in one fist and holding the umbrella handle with the other. "Listen to me! I want to quit my job at the department store. Really. I will do it. It means nothing to me. You can get a fulltime job at the art school or anywhere, I know you can. You were so popular there. You are a brilliant teacher, darling. We'll take a vacation, to Europe or somewhere. To Ireland."

"Yeah, now there's a great idea," he said sarcastically. "That's all I need. No, the door to that past is definitely shut forever."

"All right. To America, then. You have never been to New York. The museums there will be an inspiration to you. The Frick, the Museum of Modern Art, the Guggenheim. I was there the summer before we met."

"Drop it, will you? There's no need to go anywhere. I'm perfectly happy here. And besides, where are we going to get the money, eh? I bring in nothing."

"I'll get severance pay. It would be a lot. After we get back from our vacation, you could start teaching. They would pay you a high salary because you're a foreigner and so popular. It's a good idea, Nick."

Nick looked down at her.

"And what then?"

"What do you mean, what then?"

"What do we do after you quit, we go on our vacation and I start teaching art? What then?"

"What then? We can go back to the way we once were. You remember. We can act without thinking about everything all the time, what is going to happen next week, next month, next year. We just go on with our life. We...live."

"Uh-huh."

"And I would really take it easy and I could get pregnant again. I'd stay in bed nine months if it meant keeping the baby."

Suddenly Nick let go of the umbrella, which teetered momentarily until Setsuko tightened her grip on the handle.

"It's not going to happen!" he shouted.

"Shhh, people will hear you."

"People? Who? There's nobody here. There isn't a soul

around us, Setsuko. Who the fuck cares!"

He rarely calls me by my name, she thought, and now in such an angry tone.

"I'm sorry."

"Yeah, sorry. Sorry for what, eh? Remember what the doctor in Kyoto said? You can't have any more children, Setsuko. You had our two. There won't be any more, full stop."

"Just because one doctor says it, it doesn't make it true."

"You nearly bled to death."

"I don't care! I don't goddamn care! I'm bleeding to death now, Nick."

Setsuko could no longer hold back the flow of tears and she began to sob uncontrollably. But Nick did not comfort her, did not move to touch her, as he might do for an acquaintance or even a stranger. He just stood there staring across the tracks.

"Are you through now?" he said.

"Yes."

"You can't have another child. There will be no more. So just leave it. Oh, we'll go on, don't you worry about that. We will go on, that's for sure."

By the time they arrived home the rain had let up. Nick opened the front door, shaking out the umbrella, closing it and putting it in its ceramic stand. Setsuko went to the toilet, where she remained for half an hour, then trudged through the studio, passing by Nick who was seated motionless at his workbench, removed her dress and climbed into bed, pulling the sheet over her mouth.

Nick eventually stood up and undressed in his studio, laying his clothes on a cleared area of the workbench. He walked naked through the apartment to the toilet, lifted the lid and urinated, looking at himself in the mirror all the while. He returned to his studio and stood by his workbench, staring into the bedroom, where he could see Setsuko looking at him, the sheet pulled tautly across her mouth like a gag, only her nose, eyes, forehead and hair visible. He entered the bedroom, opened the dresser drawer, took out the bottoms of his worn silk pajamas, put them on and got into bed, lying on his side with his back to her.

Suddenly he felt her hand on his shoulder, then against the middle of his back. Slowly the hand moved around his torso, resting gently on his belly.

"Nick," she said. "Nick."

Her hand moved down, lightly touching his genitals.

"Stop it," he said, taking her hand in his and placing it on the strip of sheet between them. "Get your hands off me."

At least he touched me, she thought, and thinking that, was soon lost to sleep.

THE SHINJUKU ACADEMY OF ART WAS LOCATED ON A BACK street in Kabuki-cho. Not at all a district associated with art, she thought. The night clubs and bars looked particularly tawdry in the mid-afternoon sun. One barker, still in his black suit and tie from the night before, was leaning against a sign that advertised "Blond Nudes Standing on Every Table" with photos of a line of scantily clad Japanese dancers with blond hair bending sideways, forward and backward.

Squeezed between two clubs was an ultra-modern concrete building with "SINCE 1984" carved into stone alongside the entrance and a long black cloth banner hanging from a third-story window with SHINJUKU ACADEMY OF ART in calligraphic red English lettering running down it.

The automatic sliding doors opened as Setsuko approached them, and a group of young Japanese women dressed in baggy pants and tight-fitting tank tops emerged, laughing uproariously. Setsuko waited for them to pass before entering the building. She asked to see the principal, Mr. Hashizume, and was instructed to take a seat on a bright pink leather sofa in a small waiting room. Young art students carrying portfolios of various sizes were strolling in and out the building, engrossed in conversation. A shortish man of about fifty, nearly bald except for long stringy tufts of dyed-brown hair over his ears, emerged from the elevator, greeting Setsuko.

"Mrs. York," he said, taking off his rimless glasses, "what a pleasure to meet you. I am your husband's greatest fan."

"*Itsumo shujin ga osewa ni natte orimasu* (You have done so much for my husband)," she said, following the principal into a room off a corridor by the reception desk. A young woman in uniform entered with two cups of green tea on a tray, placed the tea on the table, bowed perfunctorily and left.

"How is Dr. Nick? I haven't seen him in, oh, I am sorry. I cannot tell you how deeply shocked I was..."

"Thank you very much," said Setsuko, bowing.

"Please have some tea," he said, taking a sip from his own cup and sucking air through his teeth as he drank. Setsuko merely bowed again without speaking or reaching for her cup.

"You know, we would have Dr. Nick back here in a flash. The students love him, especially the older ones who do evening classes. We are unique in Japan, you know, in that we do not discriminate by age. Art is a talent that can visit one at any age. Look at me!" he chuckled, gesturing toward her cup, adding, "Please, please, Mrs. York."

Once again Setsuko nodded her head, this time reaching halfway for her cup then withdrawing her hand.

"Well, that is what I have come to see you about, actually."

"About what?"

"Well, whether you would consider having my husband back again."

"As a teacher? Why, of course. We have four terms a year here and have just begun our autumn one. But he could start in mid-December, then even take advantage of the New Year break. It's the best term for the teachers with the least number of hours."

"Thank you. But I am enquiring now about fulltime employment, not parttime as he was doing when he was here before."

"Oh," he said, putting down his cup and sucking in air between clenched teeth. "Well, it's, uh, easier, you see, to hire him on an hourly basis. The pay isn't bad that way either, you know."

"Oh dear, please, I was in no way complaining about the pay," she said, now taking her cup in one hand and resting it in the palm of the other.

"I understand. But, you see, this is a business like any other. Full employment in this country, as you know very well, implies a commitment to the employee for, well, if not exactly for life, at least for a long time."

"Oh, I assure you that my husband can justify that commitment."

"I understand. Has this request come from your husband himself?"

Setsuko put the cup to her lips. There was still some steam rising from the tea and she felt it, like breath, against her face.

"He is very committed to his art, as you know. I am sure that he would throw himself into such a job with heart and soul."

"Yes, I am sure. Well, thank you very much for taking the trouble to come to see me," he said, standing abruptly. "Not many of our graduates will actually become artists, you know. Very very few, if any. In fact, we have never had one. But, having a practicing artist like your husband around here would certainly be an encouragement to our students."

"Thank you very much. You have been so kind to take the time to see me, what with your busy schedule."

"Busy? Me? I'm poor and idle. Got to be. Have to set an example to the students, you know!"

The principal guffawed, a hand holding onto his rimless glasses. He led Setsuko out of the room, saying *"Dozo dozo* (Please, please)" to her as she went through the doorway.

What is leading me from one place to another, she thought, what gives me the strength to get on a train, walk through a doorway, so much as lift a cup of green tea? Am I contriving this, going from one building to another, seeing people and asking them questions? Why confront them with questions, requests, plotting? Does it matter what answer they give? Are other people part of what I am doing, plotting this with me, politely peering through my designs?

Setsuko stood alone in the narrow street in front of the night club beside the Shinjuku Academy of Art. The barker, exhausted, was still leaning against his sign, now looking her way, winking. He smiled wistfully and shrugged his shoulders.

NICK WAS ALONE IN THE KITCHEN, SITTING AT THE TABLE fingering an oval Oribe bowl with edges curved up into a smooth wide lip, picking up a morsel of sea urchin from it on the tip of his black lacquered chopsticks, holding it in the air, staring into space for a long moment, then replacing it in the bowl. He drank down cold sake in his sake cup.

"This is ko-kutaniyaki (old Kutani ware)," Prof. Shiomi had

said to Nick, when he gave him the large *guinomi* sake cup in Kyoto years before. "My grandfather was from Kanazawa and we found this in his godown after his death. Now it's yours, York. *Guinomi* are larger than your usual sake cups. A *guinomi* is a 'gulper.'"

The television in the kitchen was tuned to *Ryori Tengoku* (Food Paradise), and Yoshimura Mari was hovering over a portly man in a navy-blue blazer who was about to deposit a succulent slice of lobster into his mouth.

"Isn't this amazing!" she said. "Ryuko-san, have you ever seen lobster prepared like this, poached in a paper bag dipped in boiling spa water? It's what you would expect from the master chefs of Beppu. Isn't it amazing!"

Ryuko-san, an ex-sumo wrestler, popped the lobster into his mouth, chewed for a moment with his lips tightly closed, a consummately blank expression on his face, swallowed it and looked up briefly at Yoshimura Mari, flashing a wry smile at her.

"He approves. Isn't it amazing!" she screeched, with both arms raised in the air.

Nick poured himself another cupful of sake.

A man must have a title, he thought, and what is mine? Sculptor, no, Ex-Sculptor. Perhaps I could get a job on Food Paradise, they have had foreigners on the program. I have seen them. All you need is a face in this country, a face that makes you a character. Be a character, like Charlie Brown or Felix the Cat, and you become a white-face somebody for the Japanese. Stop this, Nick, he said to himself, this cynicism will kill you once and for all. Better to drink it through and stop thinking. He poured another sake for himself, but the gulper overflowed, spilling sake onto the table top, a thin stream of it running along the polished surface until it reached the edge. Ex-Something-or-Other is not a title. Let me think. Irish Expatriate. No, won't do. Ex-Lecturer. Ex-Husband. No. Occasional husband. When the occasion warrants. No, I got it. Ex-Father. Try that on for size!

Nick bolted up, as if startled by some strange noise in the next room, leaned over the table, drained the cup of its sake with a jerk of the head, switched the television onto mute, pulled a piece of paper out of his jeans pocket, reached for the phone and pressed the buttons. He heard her voice, a message in Japanese. She was out. He was about to hang up but, reconsidering, left a message.

"Uh, hi, this is Nick York. Sorry to find you out, I mean, I guess you're not in, so, anyway, I thought I'd call and maybe, well, we could go to see Lafcadio Hearn's body or something. Just kidding. Not really interested in his body. But, well, give us a call if you, I mean, want to, or..."

After that he left his number and hung up. He glanced at the television screen and turned the sound back on. Yoshimura Mari, with the footwork of a boxer, was now moving about behind a table, hovering over three celebrity guests who were eagerly devouring the various Kyushu delicacies that had been prepared on the show. With her hands now clasped against her chest, as if in prayer, she was shaking her head, exclaiming, "Isn't it amazing!" Nick turned the television off.

The only sound in the room he could hear now came from the ticking of the wall clock over the refrigerator. He pushed the kitchen chair back, poured himself another sake, drank it down, put the *guinomi* on the table and walked toward Emi's room. He stood on the threshold. The room was surprisingly clean and fresh, as if it had been lived in, not just left in that state for a year and a half. The bed, the little desk with her comic books, the mirrored closet, the altar with her photograph and her stuffed parrot now moved into her room. I am going to do it, he thought, this is the right time. After all, a year and a half has gone by, nearly one-fourth of a lifetime for her.

Nick entered the room and touched the surface of the closet mirror with his fingertips. His fingers shaking, he pressed them against the mirror. It felt strangely warm to the touch. He slid the door open. The sleeve of her red jacket suddenly slipped out of the closet, and Nick jumped, as if given an electric shock. He gently stroked the arm of the jacket. The sleeve felt somehow rough, like fine sandpaper. He pushed the sleeve back into the closet, closing the sliding door with his toe, then turning around, approached her bed, gradually pulling the blanket off her pillow. He lay down in her bed, resting his head on her pillow. Emi had preferred a soft pillow and his head sunk deeply into it. Oh no, he thought, now comes this terrible flow of liquid, up from my gut, through my esophagus, not into my throat but into the back of my nose and then up and out my eyes. I can feel the flow, follow its burning. Acid. Oh God. Mustn't allow this to happen. He began to wheeze, gasping for breath, then the tears flowed onto the pillowcase. The phone rang. He bolted up, gasping for a breath, wiped his face on his shirt sleeve and ran into the kitchen.

"Hello."

"Oh hello, Nick-san? This is Yuko Maeno. I am so sorry. I went out shortly. Now I am back here and I heard your call."

"Oh, thank you, well, I..."

"It would be nice if we can go to the cemetery at Zoshigaya, not Soshigaya."

"Yes, I know."

"Please, I am just pulling your legs. It is a joke."

"Yes, I know."

There was a long pause.

"Hello?" she said.

"Yes, hello."

"Oh. Hello. I do wish to meet you again. Do you wish to meet me again, Nick-san?"

"Well, yes, um, I do. I telephoned you," said Nick, holding the receiver between his neck and shoulder while pouring sake into his *guinomi.*

"How about next Wednesday?"

"Um, Wednesday is not so good really. Any other day. *Kayobi*?"

"Tuesday? Sometimes I forget you are not Japanese, Nick-san. That would be exceedingly fine. Can I say that?"

"Yeah. Great. Where should we meet?"

"There are many entrances to the cemetery so that is no good. Can you meet with me at the Seibu Department Store in Ikebukuro? They have a great music shop there with tapes from all over the world. I will be in that shop at one in the afternoon on Tuesday."

"So will I."

"Thank you. Goodbye, Nick-san."

"Bye, Yuko."

Nick replaced the receiver and went to his studio. Some weeks before, he had purchased a set of chisels and a few blocks of wood. The wood had been cut and left outside to age at a farm at Kiryu, in Gunma, for five years. He took a wide-bladed chisel out of the rolled canvas bag and held it in front of his face, touching its curved edge with his fingertip. It is the first cut that establishes the art, he thought. The most subtle expression, the finest detail is set in the very first thrust of the chisel into the block of wood. Everything after that is adjustment.

He picked up a large mallet and banged the end of his chisel deeply into the wood, creating a gash that ran more than half the length of the block. A shaving, though quite heavy, sailed into the air. There was something resembling a smile on his face as he watched the shaving fall, the first smile for as long as he could remember.

TUESDAY CAME, A COOL OCTOBER DAY, AND CROWDS OF women were milling in the boutiques of Isetan, half a handbag full of 10,000-yen bills, their single mind focused on the brands before their eyes. What are they really seeking, Setsuko thought. No, I mustn't think like this, if I do, I will lose my will to work here. She waited with Arai Toshiyuki in a corner, watching the lines of women intertwine, threads that crossed and easily unraveled, joining again in another spot. YOUR AUTUMN EXTRAVAGANZA!!! read the sign in gold English lettering, hanging between two tall pillars. "The theme of retailing in Japan today is excess," she had said at a meeting in June, when creating the slogan for the campaign. An excess of everything. Now, four months later, I have finally come to realize that I myself have been surviving on its opposite, on lack, inadequacy and the scattering of feeling.

"In a way, it's funny," said Arai Toshiyuki. "I somehow feel as if we're not all that needed anymore, like parents who can sit on the sidelines and merely observe their children from now on."

"What do you mean?" asked Setsuko.

"Well, I mean, look at these customers. They are moving about, weaving among each other, stopping only to examine a garment for a moment until they throw it over their arm like a dish towel, one on top of the other, garments costing 50,000, 70,000 or 100,000 yen each. They don't need to be guided anymore. They have enough momentum, and money, in them to last them, and us, for some time to come."

"Isn't that a good thing?"

"Yes, I'm thrilled, really. So should we all be. We have created a kind of prosperity in this country that is unprecedented. I just wonder how long it is really going to last."

"According to the section chief, a minimum of a thousand years."

"Oh yes, I forgot," he chuckled. "What worries me is what all this is leading up to."

"What do you mean?"

"I mean, what are the lives of these women like? Is all this buying going to miraculously give them what they want and need?"

"What?" said Setsuko. "No one ever said that shopping was a substitute for self-fulfillment. We're not in that business. Not yet, at least."

Until then the two of them had been conversing without eyes meeting, staring to one side then another, and now Setsuko peered into his eyes. A kindly-looking man, she thought, with a soft self-deprecating expression and an inquisitive, even playful, smile. What would draw such a man to a job like this, she wondered, why hadn't he chosen a life with a higher purpose?

"Would you have coffee with me after work today or...?" he said, tightening the knot in his necktie.

"Sorry, what was that?"

"Uh, oh, never mind, I just thought..."

"Coffee?"

"Well, just to discuss, I mean, the next year's spring collection, that's all."

"I can't today."

"Sure, I understand."

A look of shyness fell over his face and he blushed, gazing downward.

"I have to go somewhere today," she said. "I was hoping to be able to get away early today, for this family thing, but instead of going home I could meet you tomorrow though, say, around 7:30, I mean, only if you want."

"That's, uh, fine, yes. There's a wine bar, recently opened, on the Ginza, behind the Hattori Clock Building."

"I haven't been there, but I'm sure I can find it. What's it called?"

"Za Chateau. I'll be there at 7:30."

"Za Chateau. Got it. So will I," said Setsuko.

I can smile at him, nodding pleasantly. I can feel the furrows in my forehead. I am surprised that any man would wish to have a drink with me.

Setsuko stepped onto the escalator. Arai Toshiyuki watched her descend, calling to her, "I'll tell Section Chief Saito you've left a bit early for family reasons."

Now between floors, she turned halfway around, smiled again and bowed to him. Don't want to show my face now, this stretched-canvas, whitish mask that I display to everyone, this ghost's countenance with its wan excuses for expression. It is not *muhyojo* (impassive), she thought, it is drawn and fixed, reacting mechanically as the occasion warrants to every little challenge. I am duty-bound to execute one sure action after another, as if a woman's only virtue was the virtue of continuation.

Setsuko paused briefly at the Chanel counter, bought a bottle of Chanel No. 5 on impulse, emerged from the department store and walked swiftly under the railway bridge by Shinjuku Station in the direction of the Ome Highway. She had phoned

Mr. Hashizume at the art school and been given the address for the house. She walked along the highway for some fifteen minutes, turning off it to the right into a one-lane side street. The district of boulevard and skyscraper was immediately transformed into a grid of back alleys and drab shacks. She took a few turns and arrived at an old wooden house with a covered gate. She stopped to catch her breath. The gate was blanketed in a trellis of bush clover, and this thick meshing of lattice, leaf, stem and flower against a blank light-blue sky caused her to gasp for a breath. Is this the answer to beauty then, she thought, is it in these old splintered planks with no paint, no varnish, no protection, just weathering, not fighting the hard push of time but rather adorning the decay it brings in a blend of texture and color?

Attached to one of the wooden pillars of the gate was a white stone nameplate with the name carved in black cursive writing. SHIOMI TOKUNOSUKE. Setsuko entered the gate and approached the front door.

"*Gomen kudasai* (Excuse me)," she said, sliding the rickety front door open. The entryway was dark, and it took a moment for her eyes to adjust to the contrast with the outside. "Excuse me," she repeated.

"*Hai, tadaima* (I am coming)."

Gradually Setsuko could make out the outlines of a steep narrow staircase and a figure emerging from the dark corridor beside it, at first a vaguely white vertical rectangle, then a gray oval above it and finally the figure itself, a woman standing on the polished wooden floor, smiling, and the same voice saying, "I am terribly sorry to have kept you waiting."

The woman sat on her knees, bowing her head and placing the middle three fingers of both hands together on the floor in front of her. "Welcome," she said, raising her head, now with a more generous smile than before.

"Please excuse my rudeness for coming without telephoning and without so much as bringing a gift."

"Oh, please don't mention it. We have so few visitors these days. I am very happy that you have come. Besides, we have no telephone here. Father hates all 'contraptions,' as he calls them."

"I am the wife of one of your father's former students. My husband, Nicholas York, holds your father in very high regard. Your father was an inspiration to my husband and many others."

"Thank you very much. It is very kind of you to say so. Actually, Father is told that by many of his former students. He so enjoyed teaching. I think that he considered it his life's work, over and above his own creating. At any rate, please do come in."

Setsuko hesitated. I have come to plead a case, she thought, and it is I who should be bowing down to this woman who obviously has dedicated her life to someone, to a man, one man, father, husband, there is no difference, even son I suppose.... What would that have been like?

"Thank you very much. Well, just for a few moments perhaps."

Setsuko removed her shoes, placing them neatly together beside a large roughly hewn stone, and stepped onto the raised floor.

"This way, please," said Prof. Shiomi's daughter, leading Setsuko into a waiting room with a wave of her palm.

"What a lovely house you have," said Setsuko.

"Oh, surely you are joking. I was born in this house sixty-one years ago, you know. It was built in the early Taisho era and nothing has been altered. Well, I am nearly from the Taisho era myself," she laughed to herself, "as you can readily see. No one wears these *appappa* (long one-piece aprons) anymore. Father favors it, so I wear it to please him. This was my mother's, actually. It has been repaired here, see the stitching? Father doesn't mind my repairing clothing here and there, but he believes that everything that is standing should fall apart of its own accord, given time. 'Time is the best judge,' he always says, but, you know, I don't think he means it the way other people do. Other people think things that last are valuable. Father believes things that crumble, fall to pieces and vanish are valuable. Well, he does."

They were now standing in the small, stuffy waiting room that contained a low rosewood table and two enormous old armchairs covered in chintz cloth with faded beige antimacassars.

"Please wait here," she said, bowing, leaving and shutting the door behind her.

There was one window in the room. Its tarnished brass clamp was tightly shut. Where does the air come from to this room, she wondered. When was the last time someone sat in this room and for how long? The dull-brown earthen walls had naturally shed a considerable amount of their powdery surface, and the wide horizontal wooden skirting had lost its finish. Two oil paintings in simple wooden frames hung on the walls. Setsuko recognized them as medieval European scenes, but could tell no more. Above her head was a dim yellowish light in a cloth shade, four faded crimson tassels dangling down from it.

"Excuse me," came the professor's daughter's voice, and with that the brass knob turned and the door opened. She entered carrying a red lacquered tray. On the tray were a cup of green tea and a *yokan* (sweet bean-jelly cake) on a small flat

Mashiko plate.

"Oh, thank you," said Setsuko, bowing.

"I am sorry to have kept you waiting."

She put the tray on the low table and, with a steady hand, placed the tea cup and *yokan* in front of Setsuko.

"I am afraid that this is all we can offer you. I am sorry."

"Oh no, I am sorry for having visited unannounced."

Once again Setsuko bowed.

"Please, do have some *yokan* and tea. Father is very partial to *yokan*, you know. He once said that his favorite color in the world is *yokan* color."

"I am not sure what you mean."

"This dark-brown, purplish color. He once joked that had he remained in Europe he was considering changing his name to Juan Yokan. You have heard, I am sure, of Juan Gris. It was Father's way of getting the upper hand on the Europeans."

She giggled to herself, covering her mouth with her hand. Setsuko cut into the *yokan* with the small wooden two-pronged fork that was on the plate, and put a slice in her mouth. Then, while chewing, she took a sip of tea, staring into the two dark pictures on the wall.

"I don't believe that I have had the pleasure of meeting your husband," said Prof. Shiomi's daughter. "But Father has had so many foreign admirers. He always says that the Japanese are 'cavemen with berets on' when it comes to art. They put on Western pretenses, stare at a canvas and paint like primitives, striving for nothing more than a result that looks like something that has had earlier success, preferably in Europe. 'A nation of derivative cavemen,' that's what Father always calls the Japanese."

Again she twittered, stifling her laugh by pressing her fingertips against her lips.

"I would like to ask your father a small favor, actually," said Setsuko, putting down her tea cup. "It is very presumptuous of me."

"You must excuse my going on and on about Father. He speaks so little these days, I suppose that I feel I must speak for him."

"He is lucky to have a daughter so devoted to him."

"Lucky? I never thought of it that way. People of my generation had no choice. It doesn't occur to us that there is an alternative to devotion."

"I see."

"You are young, Mrs. Yo-ru-ku. Did I say that correctly?"

"Yes."

"You are the lucky one."

Setsuko reached for her handbag on the floor beside the armchair, pulling out a small white envelope. She opened the envelope, producing a packet of color photographs, which she placed on the table in front of the professor's daughter.

"These are some of my husband's recent sculptures. I am not a very good photographer, I am afraid, and I fear that I haven't done them justice. But I do believe that my husband is very talented, not only as a sculptor but also as a teacher."

The daughter tentatively touched an edge of the packet of photographs, immediately withdrawing her hand.

"Oh, I can in no way look at these. You see, I am no judge of art whatsoever. Only Father can do that."

"Well, I was hoping that I might see him for a brief moment to show him these. I am sure that Prof. Shiomi would remember my husband. Then I was hoping, and once again you must forgive my presumptuousness, that Prof. Shiomi would be kind enough to write a recommendation for my husband, so that he could get a fulltime job at a university or a junior college. It would not even have to be one in Tokyo. It could be in Kyoto or anywhere. We are prepared to move anywhere in Japan. My husband and I would be eternally grateful to your father."

The daughter looked into Setsuko's eyes, cleared her throat and bowed her head.

"Thank you very much," she said. "It is kind of you to think of Father at such a time. Of course it would certainly be possible. But, you see, Father is not at all well."

"Oh, I am sorry to hear that. Perhaps then just a quick call. Oh, or if there is no telephone, perhaps you might convey the message to him to help."

Setsuko paused, as if interrupted by the daughter's severe and intense stare, now finding the closeness of this room unbearable. She started to take short breaths while trying to conceal the merest hint of anxiety. I must have this recommendation, she thought. It is imperative.

"You see," said the professor's daughter, "Father had a stroke in the summer. I am afraid that he has still not regained his speech or much of his movement. I am taking care of him as best as I know how. I wish that I could speak for him, but I know nothing about these matters, you see, only what Father tells me."

The air in the room felt more stifling and close than before. How does this woman continue to breathe, thought Setsuko, how does she function so perfectly, doing exactly what is expected of her without guidance? Is it her nature to do so? Oh, to be born with such a nature, imbued with devotion, disciplined by a natural sequence of events!

Setsuko slid the photographs back toward herself and replaced them in her handbag. She rose, steadying herself by grasping the arm of the chair.

"*Ojama shite kyoshuku desu* (I am very sorry for disrupting you)," she said. "Please give my best regards to Prof. Shiomi and my hopes for a speedy recovery."

"That is very kind of you. Thank you very much," she said, opening the door.

A rush of cold air hit Setsuko's face and she took a deep breath of it, exhaling a sigh.

"Well, I will go now."

"Thank you. Please wait one moment," said the daughter, walking slowly toward the entryway and turning the corner into the corridor.

Setsuko knelt in the entryway, placed her shoes on the stone, stepped down from the raised floor and slipped into them. Hearing a low creaking noise she turned toward the corridor.

From the darkness she saw the figure of a man in a wheelchair emerge, first his knees wrapped in a checkered travel rug, then his face with a fixed grim expression, neither angry nor sad. He wheeled his chair forward with short mechanical pushing of the left hand, his right arm flush against his side with the hand, palm up, resting in his lap. Behind him his daughter, not pushing the chair but nonetheless coming forward with it, she too staring fixedly at Setsuko with the same expression of impassive determination that was written on the face of her father.

"Well, goodbye," said Setsuko, bowing and turning about, sliding the front door open and shut, not raising her head high enough to see the professor and his daughter watching her leave.

Now it was a contrast in reverse, the movement from the dark into the blinding light, so much so that it made the outside painful to look at, until gradual detail, first gray, then whitish, then yellow, then brightly colored, filled in the picture, the path of stones, each set into the ground on a different angle from the one before, each a different size, leading from the front door, the sides of the house itself, cracked boards, rusted nails sticking out here and there, the roof's crooked tiles, some chipped or broken yet somehow remaining together, the back of the gate with almost no leaves or stems or bush clover flower, the entire trellis facing the front, the house itself boasting no decoration whatsoever, the back of a canvas and frame, betraying no hint of what is seen from the street, the sky still a featureless sheet. How did all this pass into the present, she wondered, how did this little scene survive the merciless destruction of the war, the decades of growth and prosperity and drastic change all around it? Why on earth is this still here?

NICK CAUGHT SIGHT OF YUKO IN A DOORWAY NOT FAR FROM the department store music shop, torso nearly facing him full on, her head twisted around in profile against the tinted glass of the shop window, her right hand, with fingers spread, resting on her hip, half Renoir, half Picasso, he thought, transfixed for a moment by an erotic coincidence of curved and straight line. How long has it been since those lines have had a third dimension for me, have been a thing that I can reach out and touch, he thought. Oh God, York, you are succumbing, yes, your eyes are shutting involuntarily, your breathing is becoming intermittent, like that of a sick man in hospital, your skin, it has a lizard's coldness, numb as stone. She is rotating her head in my direction ever so slowly, her fingers gripping the bone of her hip and I still have time to walk away from this, to meet her in the music shop or not at all, or see an old grave with her and call an end to it there. I still have a few seconds before our eyes meet and she will be facing me, both hands on her hips, lips parted, staring straight into me.

"Hi," she said, walking toward him. "I was just being diverted over there. Are you waiting a long time?"

"No, just got here," he said, clearing his throat and rubbing the stubble on his chin.

She was dressed in jeans, tight-fitting tie-dyed tan blouse, black satin jacket and black sneakers. "I was just listening to a poetry reading by Shiraishi Kazuko," she said, smoothing the satin sleeve of her jacket with the back of her hand. "She read while two black American jazz musicians played music, saxophone and cello. They are trying to save the whales."

"Oh, whales, yeah. Great."

There was an awkward pause as the two stood in the middle of the floor. The event had ended and young couples from the audience were streaming past them. I have got one more chance, he thought, keep the conversation on whales, don't go beyond whales and you will be safe.

"Come along," she said, taking his arm in hers and leading him toward the escalator before he had another moment to think. "We'll get nowhere standing here like this."

It was nearing four when they arrived at an entrance to Zoshigaya Cemetery. A freezing wind was sweeping the path, carrying the first fallen leaves of the season toward them. Yuko pulled her jacket closed, zipping it up.

"Here, have this," said Nick, taking the muffler off his shoulders and offering it to her.

"Oh, oh, okay, thank you."

She wound the muffler around her neck, tying it at the side, once again taking his arm in hers and leading him into the cemetery.

"Whose body should we see first?" she asked.

"Whose body? You mean, well, you lead me to whatever body takes your fancy."

Yuko, a coy smile on her lips, clutching his arm to her side, marched him from Natsume Soseki to Kindaichi Kyosuke, from Izumi Kyoka to Nagai Kafu, translating inscriptions on stones, explaining influences and era, quoting passages in Japanese that Nick could not understand but nonetheless listened to with attention, and all the while she will not let go of my arm, pulling me along as if I was a faithful animal, gripping my bicep and excitedly quoting her lines, enticing me with grimaces and little shrieks of joy.

"Kafu was the most sensual of them all," she said, picking up a Japanese maple leaf, its color only half turned, and pressing it against the front of her jacket. "There is not much concrete content in his literature to speak of, but the style is pure sensuousness, light, deeply suggestive. Can real art have almost no content, yet be utterly beautiful in its presentation? You can almost touch the skin of his prose."

"Ah."

"You are a silent man, Nick, aren't you."

"I suppose so."

"I suppose that you have had many Japanese girlfriends, I mean, before you were married."

"Not really."

She stretched out her hand and touched his cheek with the knuckles of her index and middle fingers. I barely feel the touch, the skin of my face is rough and cold, insensitive, like canvas, her hand hangs before my eyes, as if unattached to anything, as if I was able grasp it, hold it firmly against my cheek and my mouth, putting the fingers in and closing my lips around them. He suddenly looked through her long thin fingers fanned in front of his face. He grasped her hand in his and pressed her fingertips against his open lips. She did not resist. He was gripping her wrist, his thumb and middle finger fitting easily around it.

"Nick," she said, suddenly surrendering all strength in her hand.

"Now, where is this bleedin' Irishman I've come to see?" he said, smiling at her and releasing her hand.

"Okay, follow me."

She walked ahead of him now with a gradually quickening pace, turning off the path, winding around gravestones of varying heights and shapes, back onto another path, virtually jogging at one point, as if playing a game with him.

Is she trying to lose me here or force me to come after her, he thought, standing still, shuffling his feet in place, looking around for her. Yuko was nowhere to be seen and Nick was surrounded by Japanese writing in stone and untended brush, directly before him three graves in a small plot with an overhanging tree to mark them.

"This is where he is," said Yuko, appearing without warning from behind.

I could so easily turn around and take her in my arms, there is not a soul in sight, a fitting place for a kiss, in front of the grave of my ex-countryman, my ambiguous predecessor, Lafcadio Hearn, illustrious ex-Irishman in Japan, I care nothing for this compatriot, for this setting, for these trees, this season, its trumped-up meaning, its hackneyed symbolism, it is only a ruse, a gross artifice, wool pulled over the dull observer's eye, delicate wool, yes, wool designed to stupefy and fool. I care nothing for the loss that all this represents, as if bleating passionately for something fragile or half vanished will make you appear sensitive in your own eyes, convince you that you alone are attuned to the subtle little clicks of culture, uniquely receptive to the wind's silent notes, to the vulgar elegance in your life that you purport to see in the passage of time. It's all a sham! There is no message here for me. Not a single one.

"Nick, let go, you're hurting me," said Yuko, pulling her hand out of his.

"I'm sorry, Yuko. I got carried away, I guess."

"Fine," she said, taking a step backward, holding her hand against her chest.

"I'm really sorry."

"It doesn't bother me, Nick," she said, now taking his left hand and bringing it to her chest. "You just looked really funny for a moment."

"So this is your man, eh?" said Nick. "This is your Irishman."

"This is him. This is Hearn, his Japanese wife and son, who was a 'half.'"

Nick was now elated, as if the dying down of the wind had somehow cleared the air for him, and he took notice of Yuko on the path and the jagged line of gravestones, each from a different time, up and down steps with no destination, defying any perspective, and abruptly he thought, it all makes sense to me not because there is a pattern in these rising and falling gravestones, but because I can see them all together at once, vivid in every minute detail, as part of a single picture without design or pattern, peering over her head, rotating my gaze around and back, taking absolutely everything in at a single glance...and I will hold her tightly to me, not kissing her face, just grabbing her, to pull her away from this picture, to make her part of myself as observer, someone not in the picture.

"Oh, Nick," whispered Yuko, wrapping her arms tightly around his waist and letting all the resilience in her body go.

SETSUKO HAD COME OUT OF THE SUBWAY AT SUKIYABASHI by a few minutes after seven. She looked up. The sky was threatening a light autumn shower, and she caught sight of a tall banner flapping in the wind by the top floor of Printemps. IT CAN BE YOURS! AS NEVER BEFORE! IT CAN BE ALL YOURS! Slogans like mine, she thought, just like the clever words created by me giving permission to possess happiness, allowing people to say to themselves, "I can be somebody else when I have this, I can conceal the emptiness inside me with this radiant object in my possession." She walked toward the Hattori Clock Building and turned left into a side street. A sign, "Za Chateau B1," indicated that the wine bar was in the basement.

Arai Toshiyuki, already seated at the long zelkova-wood counter, saw Setsuko enter. He beckoned her to the stool next to him.

"*Irrashaimase* (Welcome)," shouted several young men decked out as French country waiters, each with a name tag in fancy arabesque-style letters that read GARÇON TARO and GARÇON KAZUYUKI.

"Hello," he said.

"Hello."

"What would you like?"

"Whatever you are having," Setsuko replied, sitting beside him.

Arai Toshiyuki downed his glass of the remaining red wine and raised a finger into the air. "Another half bottle of Chateau Margot."

"*Oui, kashikomarimashita* (Oui, immediately, sir)."

"Chateau Margot? Isn't that expensive?"

"I'm living in a house inherited from my parents, I've got no loan, no wife, I never see the boys. Clothes and wine are my sole luxuries. Look, you must be hungry."

"No thank you. I don't feel like eating right now, Arai-san."

"Please, call me Toshi and I'll call you Setsuko-san."

"All right, Toshi-san, how do you do? I mean, no that's a funny thing to say," she let out a giggle, like a little girl, adding, "I mean, of course it's fine."

Over the two hours that they sat at the counter Setsuko poured her heart out to him. What is the right way to convey this to him, she thought, am I confined by people close to me, trapped in a dull interval, or have I reached a dead end, the path fallen away, my feet on the edge of a tall cliff, or is this all just something much more mundane and ordinary, a common every day like everyone else's, no alarm, no dreadful illusions, no predestination of the wicked or the banal, just one moment after the next without the prospect of joy? What's so strange about that? Is my life really different from that of other women? So, I will tell him all about the death of my precious daughter, Emi, the distance between me and my husband, the utter coldness, unrelenting, the silences that rack my brain, and in telling this man, who gazes tenderly at me, forgivingly, I am supposed to feel that a burden has lifted off my shoulders, the secret burden of misery, tedious pity kept all along to myself, the helplessness that only I have known, yes, the helplessness of nursing emotions and getting nothing given in return for it, in telling this man I am supposed to feel relief, a flash of comfort, a drop of a tear in his compassionate eyes on my skin. But at the end of the pouring out my life to him, I feel nothing. Perhaps nothing is precisely what I am aiming for.

"I don't know what to say," he sighed, fiddling with the stem of his glass.

"There is nothing you can say. I wasn't fishing for sympathy."

"Oh, I know that. But, Setsuko-san, I am deeply, deeply

moved by what you have told me. You are an amazing woman, I can tell you that. You have such strength in you, much more than I do in me. After my wife's, well, death I, sort of, went to pieces. Still haven't recovered, I guess. The only good thing is that the boys, who positively despised me throughout their teens and wouldn't so much as give me the time of day, instantly mellowed when she died, and we have gotten along pretty well ever since."

"With me it was the opposite. Our daughter's death ran a cleaver straight down between me and Nick, cutting us off from each other, though, I must admit, it wasn't as if we were all that close to each other before. We once were, though, once...."

Setsuko lowered her head, nearly down to the counter.

"Would you care to order more?" asked a crew-cut waiter with GARÇON NORITADA written on his badge.

"I would like to go," said Setsuko in a low voice.

"What was that?"

"I would like to leave here," she repeated.

Some moments later they were standing side by side at the top of the basement stairs. The ground was wet, but it had stopped raining.

"Where would you like to go now?" he asked.

"Any direction but one that will take us to our beloved home away from home, our department store. Oh, gosh, I think I am drunk again. Aren't women supposed to get happy when they get drunk? Perhaps it's a delayed aftereffect of alcohol and I just have to wait a few years or decades to have it. That must be it. *Mateba kanro no hiyori ari*...everything come to her who waits. Pretty good at that, I am, I am. At waiting."

Setsuko began to laugh in the back of her throat with lips closed, teetering on the stair, finding herself patting him on the shoulder rather hard, apologizing over and over again. She pleaded with her eyes, please look at me seriously and with conviction, and that look will allow me to retrieve my train of thought, to get back on its track.

He held her tightly, with both hands, at arm's length.

"Shh," he said. "I understand. Shhh, Setsuko-san."

"Let's go somewhere else. I want to go somewhere else."

They were in the back seat of a taxi heading further downtown.

"Where in Asakusa you going?" asked the driver gruffly, cocking his head on an angle.

"Uh, here will be fine."

The car screeched to a halt, he paid the driver, refusing the receipt with a wave of the hand, stepped out of the taxi and offered his hand to Setsuko. She grabbed it and felt him pull her out. This feels good, she thought, someone, a man, pulling me somewhere, taking me somewhere, and I do not want to know where, not now and not even when I get there, wherever I am taken is what I want, where I am is what I am.

The two entered a room on the second floor. There was a queen-size bed in the middle of the room with a large mirror opposite it, a dresser, a small pink desk and chair, and a television set with video cassette player.

"I'm going in there," she said, pointing to the bathroom, slightly reeling. "There."

"You're not sick, are you?"

"No. I'm fine. I'm really fine. You must think I'm an alcoholic. I never drink like this. Never."

Setsuko lifted the hem of her skirt above her waist and pulled her underwear down to her shins, staring at herself in the bathroom mirror. There was a huge round bathtub beside the toilet. Half standing, she leaned over the side of the tub, put the plug in the drain hole and turned on the hot water, losing her balance and falling back onto the toilet seat. What do I look like, she wondered, I have lost the ability to judge my appearance, I cannot imagine any person desiring to be with me, yet what is this man doing here now, what is in his mind? He has been alone for five years, yet he is so elegant and kind, many women would find him attractive, even young unmarried women, why is he here with me? Did he lure me here or have I lured him with my sob-story life and my wretched pity. I know. He is having his pity on me and demonstrating it in the guise of affection. She wiped herself and flushed the toilet, remaining on the seat, staring into the mirror. How long has it been since Nick has seen me and touched me? That cleaver...it severs every last thing in its way.

When she emerged from the bathroom he was sitting on the edge of the bed in his suit pants, white shirt and tie, a remote controller in his hands.

"Are we going to watch TV?" she asked, adjusting her skirt at the waist.

"Well, I'm not sure if this is for the TV or the bed," he said. "I've never been to a love hotel before."

"Neither have I. You've got to watch what you press around here," she said, laughing. "May I see it?"

"Sure," he said, handing the remote controller to her.

"Ah," she said, "not that I have ever seen one of these, but this is for the in-house television, I think. These buttons on the bottom let you choose in-house movies, you know. Shall we watch one?"

"Well, I don't know."

He lowered his gaze, blushing, as she turned the television on and pressed the menu button at the bottom of the remote controller. A message appeared on the screen, informing them that adult movies were charged to the account at three thousand yen each.

"I've never seen one of these," said Setsuko. "I think I feel like it. Wouldn't mind seeing other people having a good time. Do you mind?"

"Well, I really don't know," he said.

"Oh God, you're not going to say, 'Perhaps this isn't a good idea,' are you?"

"Well, I..."

"I am here because I want to be, Toshi. It is the first thing that I have done in more than a year that I can say that about. Maybe it's my first truly conscious action since then."

"Since when?"

"Since, well..."

"I'm sorry," he said, taking her hand in his.

"You're a nice man, aren't you."

"Average."

"Oh no, much more."

Standing above him she pressed her side against him, and he slowly, reluctantly, wrapped his arm around her waist, placing his cheek against her. Remaining in his embrace she rotated her body around until she was facing him and stood between his legs. He wound his other arm around her waist, his face now flush against her belly.

"Leave the television off," he said.

"I will," she said.

She knelt between his legs and they kissed. This feels so good, she thought, it is as if I have never felt a man's lips on mine, I am not going to blame myself for this, or Nick. She kissed him passionately, pulling on the knot of his tie, letting go of him for a moment, unbuttoning her blouse, removing it, unhooking her brassiere from the back, dropping it down her side to her feet. She gently pushed him onto the bed and lay on top of him, the cool smooth cloth of his white shirt against my breasts, she thought, his lovely eyes and skin, this touch.

He turned her over, rose and stood by the side of the bed, unbuttoning his shirt, shedding it, then loosening his belt and dropping his trousers. He took her hand and helped her up, and they stood face to face, kissing passionately.

"Toshi, please."

"What, Setsuko? What is it?"

"Please."

Does he know what I mean, she wondered. I cannot finish it. I cannot say another word. I want him to make me feel like some other woman, if only for a few moments of my life, a stranger to my own life, a woman who might hear of just such a story as mine and be able to say, "Well, that's sad" or "That's what happens, isn't it...but not to me!"

He drew his lips away from hers, holding her at arm's length.

"Oh, please don't stare at me like that. I must look horrible."

"No. You are exceptionally beautiful, Setsuko."

"You are not saying that to me."

"Then to who?"

"To a woman standing in front of you in a love hotel. What would Section Chief Saito say if he heard you?"

"Please don't make jokes now. Look at me. What do you see, eh? That's what I want to ask you."

"What do you mean?"

"I haven't been with a woman in five years."

"I know that. Please."

She said "please" again with the same clinging tone, an entreaty, if only he could read it.

"I can't do this," he said.

She slipped her hands off him, letting them fall limp to

her sides. "It's hard for me, too," she said. "I've never done anything like this before."

"It's not that. For the first two years after Keiko died I found myself in such deep grief I could barely function. My two boys were wonderful, they took care of me, even did my cooking and washing. They saved my life. Keiko and I were so much in love. Of course, no one at work knew. I always said the right things, you know, calling her 'the wife,' telling everybody I didn't like getting home earlier than nine. Never let on at work that my family was everything to me."

"You are always so businesslike."

"It's a disguise. What do you think? Sanehisa, he's the younger one, was terrific. He constantly urged me to get girlfriends, even to remarry. He even kept bringing me advertisements for dating agencies, you know, the kind they have in magazines. They're even doing it by computer these days apparently. I tried a few, but it didn't work. In the third year I went to a, well, um, I called an escort, I think that's what it's called, and I had a date. She was very nice, really, a married woman doing the work to put her daughter through private school. But I was unable to have sex, I mean, I couldn't, I mean, she was very nice and kind, and even after she stopped working there last year, believe it or not, I still saw her for coffee and we became great friends, her husband is a real estate agent, his office is right by Yurakucho Station, I pass it sometimes and look in and wonder which one he is."

He stopped talking. The two of them were standing face to face, at arm's length from each other.

"I understand," she said. "You have really been through a lot. I really do understand. You are a very kind man, you know that?"

"Average, really. Just plain, like every other man, no

different."

Setsuko arrived home not long before midnight. The apartment was empty. It seemed colder in it than outside. Without turning on the heater she shed her clothes and crawled into bed, shivering until the sheets turned warm.

AFTER EATING DINNER AT A KOREAN-STYLE BARBECUE restaurant behind Marui Department Store in Shinjuku, Nick and Yuko took a taxi to her apartment at Nakano Sakaue, arriving shortly after eight. They climbed the metal stairs, corroded by rust, on the outside of the building. The entire building had been encased in bamboo scaffolding, and a porous canvas-like material had been stretched around its walls. They reached the third floor and stood, for moment, between the canvas and the scaffolding. A crisscross of bamboo shadows on her face, Yuko abruptly turned about in front of him. Standing a step above him, she put her hand gently against his cheek as she had done at the cemetery.

"They've transformed us into birds in a cage," she said, reaching out for his wrist, holding it firmly against the small of her back and leading him up. "They have decided to paint this building, the owners, probably to sell it in the property boom. They're *jiageya* (property shysters), you understand? They don't ask us residents, never. One day we come home and find ourselves in a canvas and bamboo cage. Here is my flat."

She unlocked the gray metal door and entered before him, turning on the light in the entryway and producing a pair of flower-patterned slippers from the shoe cupboard. She kicked off her shoes and, stepping up onto the floor, shed her satin jacket, letting it drop to the floor. She went to the kitchen and switched on a kerosene heater with a black iron kettle perched on top of it. Nick remained in the entryway. Yuko returned to him, again taking his hand in hers and leading him forward. The door clicked shut, she bent forward and reached behind him to lock it. The side of her face brushed against his hip.

"Coffee? Tea? Or, would you like to have a beer?"

She is not at all like Japanese girls I have known, he thought. She is at ease in the company of a man in her own flat, as if I was a relative or another woman.

"Uh, I'd love a cup of tea, actually."

"Earl Grey all right? I've got Prince of Wales, if you prefer it."

"No, anything's fine."

A long purple linen *noren* curtain, split nearly in two and connected at the top, hung from the bedroom door lintel.

"What's written on this *noren*?" asked Nick, feeling the texture of the linen between his fingertips.

"What? Oh, it's just one character split in two," she said, filling an aluminum kettle in the sink. "It is the *kanji* for *jo*, passion. It was drawn by a lover, I mean, one before, in the past, that I had. He was a *noren* designer."

"I see."

"He is in Kyoto, or, I mean, he was in Kyoto. He went back to Germany last year. Wolf was his name. Don't suppose there'd be much of a market for *noren* in Hamburg."

Nick pushed a heavy glass ashtray away from him as he sat at the table.

"Do you smoke?" he asked.

"Me? Oh no. I don't smoke," she replied, shaking tea leaves from a cherrywood tea caddy into a small squarish ceramic teapot decorated in scenes of Edinburgh Castle.

I do not want to go through with this, he thought. I am being propelled from the first instant of encounter with her on the bench to this spot, the "decent" time elapsed between the two making it all appear natural and acceptable. Why not go promptly from that bench, without so much as an exchanged word, to a room, this room or one in a love hotel? What stopped that? Why the interval? It isn't as if these things do not happen between ordinary people, a stroll from bench to coffee shop, bar, restaurant leading to a dark embrace against a soft wall away from people or to obsessive lovemaking in a bed somewhere, the place doesn't matter, the reason no concern to anyone, the aim in both minds a desire for a thing that must, at any cost, be demonstrated not to the other but to the self, that the body is still a lure, that it still has the power to capture or entrap, a power that, despite all creativity, despite all passion, despite even an anarchy of imagination, can be reaffirmed and released in one way and one way only. That's what has brought me here and what is keeping me here.

"Do you like music?" she asked.

"Sure."

"Do you mind if I play a tape?"

He shook his head and Yuko disappeared through the *noren* into the bedroom. Nick looked around. The only picture on the wall was a print of Vermeer's *The Concert*, the only sound in the entire apartment now coming from the boiling of water in both the aluminum kettle on the stove and the iron kettle on the heater.

"Nick-san?" came Yuko's voice from the bedroom. "Come here for a minute, please?"

Nick hesitated, inhaled deeply, stood, turned off the gas under the aluminum kettle and, lowering his head as he pushed the *noren* apart with a loosely closed fist, entered the bedroom. Yuko was perched on the wooden rail at the foot of her bed, legs slightly spread, a small red portable cassette player in her lap.

"I can't get this thing to work," she said, pressing a button over and over again, as if irritated. "It think the bloody thing is broken."

In front of the bed there was a chair and a desk, and on the desk a Sanyo word processor and a bookshelf with books in English and Japanese. Nick squinted but could not make out titles in the gray light.

He took the cassette player from her lap, placing it on the chair's embroidered cushion and, with his hands now at her sides a few centimeters below her armpits, lifted her over the rail and gently onto the bed. This woman, who until a moment ago was a picture of self-assurance and firm poise, now lies in front of me as if every last streak of tenacity in her has been abruptly obliterated, as if the taut muscles were now suddenly transformed into the softest tissue, a hollow.

She says nothing now, certainly does not resist as the tight tie-dyed blouse is pulled over her head, the zipper at the front of her jeans is unzipped. The same force that propels me, he thought, is moving her, making her barely lift her pelvis to allow the jeans to come off. She is beautiful in her lace brassiere. I can see her nipples through the holes in the lace. I can feel her white cotton underwear. She is smiling at me with parted lips and gradually narrowing eyes. She is still.

Nick removed his clothes and laid down beside her, easily reaching around her with his right arm to unhook her brassiere at the back. Again this movement of her back off the sheet, ever so slight, allowing my hand to reach her. She is like Setsuko used to be, or is like my memory's fantasy of what used to be. Don't recall that, leave that memory where it is, deep under the layers of years, allow it to suffocate, time-gagged, until it expires. This is not Setsuko, it is Yuko beside you, York, you blooming idiot. What's happened to you? You used to do this without blinking an eye, without a care for what or who went before, you used to be able to act, and now your mind fills with pictures, details, comparisons, unable to brush away intervening time, dust stuck to an old book jacket. So rid it from your mind, deface the pictures and blot them out until everything goes blank.

He sat on his knees between her legs, pulling her underwear down her thighs and off, twisting his torso to drop them on the embroidered cushion, returning, cupping his palm, with fingers closed, exactly over her, the heel of his palm pressing into her, himself now overcome by an intensity of passion that he had not felt for...for how long? I can't remember, oh God, I can't remember any other woman at any time! I want this, I want this. I am now completely on top of her, covering her, a cloak over her entire body. Thank God, I can't remember a thing!

"I will not live without you," whispered Yuko, holding his face in her hands, then kissing his lips over and over again, her breath entering his mouth, whispering, "*Onegai*...Please, please."

Am I happy to hear this? Is the propelling of time to end with this here and now, or is there something to follow that will become a part of my life? Have I really desired this?

For the moment at least he was grateful that he could hear no answer to this in his mind.

Nick left the Chuo Line train at Suidobashi. He walked briskly to Jinbocho in the glare of the late morning sun, coming to a halt on a corner, kneeling down to pick up a golden gingko leaf and craning his neck to look up at the tree that produced it.

Can't get sentimental over a color, he thought, standing up from his crouch and brushing his knee. This is no way to mark time, time is not marked by anything outside me, I won't allow it, this tree is colorless. I won't allow time to be marked by seasons, by cheap fool's gold in the iris, the leaf's fan-like shape clipped in the middle. It means nothing, it tells me nothing about what has elapsed since the last moments or, for that matter, years of my life.

He gazed around, thinking, I must look like the worst kind of suspicious character. So be it. I will will this scene to be drained of all color once and for all, and each individual striding along this pavement will, one by one, fly off to a side, as if assaulted by an all-powerful gust of wind, a wind made of light, as if coming off the sun itself. They will sail head first, whooshed into the air, suddenly weightless, away, up and out of my sight, every last one of them. The trees will darken, branch by branch, trunk by trunk, row by row, in perfect perspective down to a distant point, transforming the entire street a monotone gray, with not a living soul as far as the eye can see...my eye, and my ideal picture in it.

Nick dropped the gingko leaf back on the ground and, placing the sole of his shoe over it, crushed it into the concrete and continued to walk toward Jinbocho, the people gradually returning to their spots and the colors of the season pouring back into their containers, their lines and planes intersecting again in his eyes. I could always close my eyes as I walk, he thought, walk as far as I can without seeing. But even if I did, I would not be able to shut out the assaulting light.

He was rifling through old art books at the Kitazawa Bookshop, leaving two of them open, side by side, on a shelf. A Giacometti bust of a woman named Isabel in bronze, a Rodin sculpture called "Eternal Lovers" in stone. Isabel Nicholas, Giacometti's lover, utterly realistic her high cheekbones, almond-shape eyes and bronze skin. He touched the glossy paper at the hollow of her cheeks. And Rodin's lovers, the man emerging from stone on his knees, his lips against her breasts, the woman kneeling above him, looking down on him, her right hand slipped down to touch her foot behind her. This liquid stone and this stretched bronze skin, I can feel them both through the surface of the paper of these books. I don't have to look at these statues to study them. Their rounded angles can be felt here, my fingertips my eyes.

Nick felt the faint rush of a breeze in the stuffy air behind him, between the high bookcases. He turned to his right, the index finger of his left hand still touching Rodin's statue. A young Western woman, nearly as tall as he, dressed in light-pink pants and a heavy-weave white wool pullover, was pirouetting on the spot and, coming full circle to face him, said, "Hello."

Nick nodded, smiling, cleared his throat and lowered his gaze to the book, shifting his hand onto the picture of Giacometti's bronze.

"I love old books. In fact, I'm here almost every day," she said, shuffling her feet like a dancer. "Can't really afford these prices, though. Much cheaper in London. American?"

The clear pronunciation and the lilt in her voice, particularly in the rising at the end of "American," marked her as English, somewhere in the Midlands, no doubt. A bizarre way to introduce yourself, he thought, with a pirouette.

"Nope. Where you from, Birmingham?"

"Gosh, how did you know?"

"Oh, it's about all I can tell these days. I got it. A ballet dancer from the Birmingham Ballet, broke a toe and ended up teaching English in Japan, both feet forward."

"Nice try. Hey, you're Irish."

"Only thing I can't hide anymore, really."

"I love Ireland, almost settled there once but, hey, you teaching English, then?"

"Nope."

"Not a teacher. What else is there?"

"Not much, I guess. Where do you teach?"

"I don't. I'm a model, for an agency in Roppongi. Want to get into television or movies or something, but I've the devil's own job convincing people that I'm more than just a pretty pair of legs."

Nick looked down at the two open books, retracting his hand. I have not seen Yuko in a fortnight, he thought. The days I spent with her, mostly at her flat, making love, listening to her tell me about Japan, about literature, holding her in my arms until she dozed off, then dressing and returning home, not exchanging any more than a rare pleasantry with Setsuko, how's work, well well, is that so? I told Yuko that I would be going overseas for some time and would get in touch again when back, and yet I spend my days walking, as if walking was a way to prepare metal, stone, clay or wood for a transformation.

"Hello?" she said, taking a step toward him. "Are you still here?"

"Oh, sorry. So, where were we?"

"Nowhere in particular. I was just telling you about myself. Look, please don't get the wrong idea, I don't go picking up stray gaijins in old bookstores, but wanna have a coffee somewhere around here? I'll even let you pay."

"Um, it's kind of you but I've got to go, really," said Nick.

"Oh. Teaching?"

"No. I'm a sculptor."

What motivated me to blurted that out, he wondered. I haven't said that to anybody since I was a student in Kyoto.

"I mean, I sculpt from time to time," he added. "Otherwise I guess you would call me a walker."

"Well, Mr. Walker, my name is Michelle. How do you do?"

She put her hand out and he took it, lightly, in his, her fingers so slim, like fine bones and nothing else.

"Very nice to meet you," he said. "But, sorry, I'm not really in very good shape now, I guess. I know that sounds awful. I mean, I don't mean it that way, it's just, um, I think I had better go."

"Yeah, I understand. I think I've been that way before. Okay. Look, here's my card. We've got to have them for the business. I'll write my home number on the back. Give us a buzz when, well, whenever, I mean, the spirit moves you."

She took a steel-colored ballpoint pen from her compact shoulder bag and wrote her telephone number on the back of her card, thrusting it forward with her long thin arm entirely outstretched and her wrist bent on a right angle. Nick took the card and, without looking at it, slipped it into the right back pocket of his jeans.

"Well, bye, Mr. Walker. I hope you can get your statues to come to life someday soon."

She crinkled her nose and, after spinning a half pirouette, sauntered between the bookcases and out the door.

Suddenly the urge to sit at his workbench and carve wood with his tools overwhelmed him and he wished he could traverse the distance between there and his home in an instant, like the pedestrians on the street who flew into the air like rice paper dolls. It is the damn colors here, he thought, accosting my eyes wherever I look, it is the damn season, the changes, without them I could move so much more evenly, undisturbed, unfettered by crisscrossing lines that I must banish from sight before taking the next step.

He saw himself walking back to Suidobashi Station, his arms flails of stone that easily repelled or felled objects in front of him. The problem is not other people, he thought, other people are not antagonistic, readily dealt with, smiled away. It's the lines that extend from objects around me, buildings, poles, signs, window panes, awnings, these stretched-out blades sticking out beyond the confines of their shape, then rushing toward me, threatening me. But they will not cut into me, not penetrate my skin, I am impervious to all things from the outside, natural or man made.

Had other people noticed Nicholas York marching the distance between Jinbocho and Suidobashi at noon on that very bright November day they would have seen a man with a confident air, and they would have said, "There goes a man with a purpose. You can see it in his walk." But Nicholas York had no purpose, save to get through the day without remembering it. My triumph, he thought, is that I am able to encounter people, new and old, without their summoning up anything that has transpired in my past life. I do not care what happens from now on because I have successfully blanked out all that went before. If this isn't happiness, then I don't know what is.

The next thing he knew he was home, it was long after noon, he was standing in the kitchen eating a large tub of "Bulgaria Yogurt" and, with the spoon sticking out of his mouth, pressing the message replay button on the telephone.

"This is Yuko," said the message. "*Gomen nasai* (I'm sorry), Nick, I had to phone you. I cannot work. I need to see you. Please." The tape went silent and Nick, thinking that the message had ended, put his finger on the erase button. "Nick, Nick, call me today," came the last words. He pressed the erase button, the machine gave off a short beep, and the tape wound back to the beginning. He put the spoon into the tub of yogurt, returned the tub to the refrigerator and telephoned Yuko, hearing a message on her phone.

"This is Yuko. Please leave a message after the beep. Thank you very much," said her voice in English, then repeating the message in Japanese.

"Hello, Yuko, it's me, Nick. Listen, I just got back home and, look, I can't have you phoning me at home, I thought that we wouldn't..."

"Hello, Nick?" said Yuko. "I'm here. I just wasn't answering."

"Oh. Well, I, um..."

"Please don't say anything. I'm sorry that I called you at your home. Please, I needed to hear your voice. I need to see you. Can you come now?"

"No. I just got back home and I'm going to work."

"Can't you work later?"

"No! I can't."

"Okay. What time is it? Oh, it's still early. You work for a while and I'll study too, and then we can meet for dinner, outside somewhere. Can you come into Shinjuku? There's a new wine bar near the NS Building, it's easy to find."

"No, Yuko, I can't. It's been a while since I have sat down and worked. I'll call you sometime, I promise."

"Don't say that, 'sometime.' I hate sometime. Nick, you can't stop seeing me. If you see me tonight I will understand and you can work after, even for a few days. You can't just stop seeing me like this."

"I'm not stopping seeing you."

"That's what you are doing. Look, you know the NS Building

in West Shinjuku, we had coffee downstairs, remember? I will be in that open area with the clock at six tonight. Okay?"

Nick paused.

"Okay," he said.

"Okay, goodbye," she said, hanging up.

He sat at his workbench, rubbing his palms over an oval piece of wood. Unrolling his chisel holder and removing a narrow straight-bladed chisel, he blew dust off the wood, rounded an edge with the tip of the blade, blowing again and carving, reducing the shape. Aha, the ultimate sculpture, he thought, reduce further and further until the last stroke of the chisel removes the thing itself, then gather the shavings and lay a thick sheet of glass over them, trapping them with all the minute dust, frame the lot, hang it on a wall and call it "An Instant in the Life of Eternal Lovers" or "Work No Longer In Progress."

The phone rang and, holding the chisel, he went to the kitchen, letting it ring, standing above it, willing it to stop. It rang on and on. Finally he picked up the receiver in the hand that held the chisel.

"Hello."

"Hello."

He didn't recognize the woman's voice.

"Hello?" he said, about to add, "Is that Yuko?"

"Hello, Nick. It's me, Setsuko," she interrupted.

"Oh."

"I'm at the store in Shinjuku, but I thought, well, I could easily buy some prepared foods in the basement and get home by about seven tonight. We've got an Italian food fair on now and they've got lots of delicious-looking things, and cheap Italian wine, too."

"I've gotta go out tonight."

"Oh."

There was a silence. I want to ask him where, she thought, but we have long ago ceased doing that, both of us. No exchanged assurances, true or not, simply the convenient tacit agreement of a married couple.

"You there?" he said.

"Okay. Well, I guess I'll just stay here then. I've got lots of things to catch up on anyway with the Christmas rush coming and everything."

"Okay, bye."

"Goodbye, Nick."

They both held the receiver to their ear for some time, each expecting the other to hang up. Should I say another word to him, she thought, should I say that I'll come home anyway? I don't care what time she comes home, he thought, but I don't want to leave this flat tonight either.

"Nick?" said Setsuko. "You there?"

Nick heard this but quickly hung up the phone, thinking, I am not going to permit anything to happen.

He carved the piece all afternoon, leaving his workbench only once to make himself a cup of coffee and go to the toilet. This would be the statue of a dancing girl, naked, standing flat footed on the floor, arms stretched above her head, fingers spread out like tiny branches, leaning forward on an angle with her chin in the air. He had finished a rough carving of the arms by the time it was dark outside, placing the piece of wood carefully in the center of his workbench and pushing the dust and the thinnest shavings into a neat pile by the edge. Then, with the back of his hand, he brushed the pile onto the floor.

He changed into his black slacks, draping his jeans over the back of a kitchen chair.

WHEN NICK ARRIVED IN THE ATRIUM OF THE NS BUILDING in West Shinjuku, Yuko was sitting on a bench beside its gigantic clock waiting for him. She caught sight of him and rushed to the middle of the atrium. They stood for a moment in silence, she taking his hand in hers and squeezing his fingers tightly.

"Where do you want to go?" she said. "I've missed you."

"To your flat."

She nodded, a big smile on her lips, and they walked through the atrium to the street where they hailed a taxi.

"The entire place smells of paint," said Nick, climbing the metal stairs ahead of her.

"They just finished painting a few days ago and took away the canvas and bamboo scaffolding. We're now at least allowed to see out of our cage."

In the entryway Nick took her in his arms and kissed her passionately, pushing her against the front door. She reached behind her back to lock it.

"Oh, Nick," she cried. "I have missed you so much. I love you."

He pressed his lips against hers with great force, his hands rubbing the small of her back until she couldn't stand there any longer. She kicked off her shoes and went into the bedroom, the *noren* brushing against her face. Nick sat on the raised floor, his knees high in the air, unlaced his boots and, half standing while pulling them off, hopped in the direction of the bedroom, flinging one boot, then another, into the entryway as he went. By the time he pushed the *noren* aside she had taken off all of her clothes and was lying on her stomach on top of the bed. He knelt by the side of the bed and began to kiss her ankles, then the inside of her knees then her thighs, gently rubbing the curve at the bottom of her buttocks as he did, Yuko beginning to moan, placing the index finger of her right hand against her lips and biting her knuckle, Nick now kissing her buttocks, winding his arms around her torso and holding her nipples between his thumb and forefinger, twisting them back and force, still kissing her buttocks, licking the small of her back, kissing the protruding bones of her hips, first one side then the other, now bringing his left hand down from her nipple over her belly to her pubic hair, rubbing her softly, his index and middle fingers separating her, gently pressing her lips there, she now raising and lowering her hips, moving his right hand away from her nipple and taking the nipple in her fingers herself, pinching it, Nick's left hand now completely over her, his index and middle fingers inside her moving up and down, his lips over her buttocks, kissing her feverishly, and she saying over and over again, "*Irete*...(Come inside me)," and he pulling off his slacks and underwear and lifting up the hem of his shirt, spreading her legs far apart and going inside her and she screaming the moment he pushes in. How long did it last? Nick had been overtaken by sleep. Waking up, it took him seconds to realize where he was.

SETSUKO ARRIVED HOME NOT LONG AFTER NINE, SAW the open tub of yogurt with the spoon sticking out in the refrigerator, the statue of the dancing girl, recognizable only as a curving block of wood with two half-formed limbs in the air, listened for messages on the phone, there were none. She picked up Nick's jeans and, taking them to the washing machine, checked the pockets. She pulled a name card from the back pocket. Written below the name Michelle was a telephone number. Ah, so that's it, she thought. Nevertheless,

I am going to retrieve something from the past. I am going to stop at nothing.

NICK STARED AT THE BLANK WALL, HIS DANCING GIRL IN his hands, its raised limbs smoother now with ball-like suggestions for hands, its legs still unseparated. Leave it now and call it done, he thought, or continue to carve and carve, head on a thin peg of neck, arms like Japanese toothpicks, legs as parallel pins leading up to wide hips. Dancer at rest? Dancer frozen in time? Or again begin to carve, reducing her to virtually nothing, carve and carve, the tissue of shavings becoming thinner and thinner, until all that is left of the whole is a pyramid of dust.

He went into the bedroom and pulled the curtains shut, returning to his studio, closing the door between it and the kitchen, making the air in there a dark medium he could cut with a slight movement of his white skin. He took out his old works in clay and stood them in a line on the floor. Then he went to the kitchen and filled a large stainless steel mixing bowl with water, carrying it back to the studio and shutting the door with his foot. The water's surface was catching all the light. One by one he drowns the statues in the glistening water, they are not so big, they make few waves, they sink to the bottom, one on top of the other, his buried soldiers, and he plunges his hands into the water, not-so-ancient pond with not-so-ancient fossils, his clay warriors that no one would bother to discover or having discovered would toss aside without a second thought. Ah, this is not reduction, he thought, it is construction, a downright reformation. This, above all, is positive, a service to art. It is no wonder that I am such an excellent cook, a baker of elegant goods, it is no wonder that people are attracted to me, given this desirable talent that I possess, this talent to crush old clay through my fingers, manipulating primal material, a god of sorts, I reckon. He didn't know which felt better, destroying his work like this or creating something out of nothing.

The statues were gone. He broke off a little ball of clay from the lump in the water, rolled it into an oval shape, and from his kneeling position in the middle of the room, flung it with all his might at the wall over his workbench. It stuck! Nick was ecstatic. York, he thought, you are brilliant. Too bad Jackson Pollock isn't alive here to see this. He swiftly created another flattened oval, this time impressing his thumb print into it, and threw it against the wall. Again it stuck! Luck strikes twice on the same wall! No, this isn't luck, it is outright genius, a virtuoso performance taking place at this very moment in Tokyo, Japan, mark the day, 30 November 1988. I'll have to sign and date this wall when I am finished, make sure that my thumbprint can be seen on it by the critics of the future. "Stillborn on the Wall" by Nicholas York. He continued this process until there was no more clay left at the bottom of the bowl. The water itself was a muddy gray. His hands were covered in a film. The wall between his studio and Emi's room was a relief of little mounds and specks spreading out from the center, orbital chaos. That is what I have created, utter chaos! Far superior to a handful of semi-realistic statues of people. Who needs a handful of semi-realistic people, people who will never come to life for anyone, not even for the man who created them? He remained for a long time in the middle of his room, his muddy pond beside him settling until the water was clear on top. He sat crosslegged, unmoving, breathing regularly, admiring his creation and waiting patiently for any one of the pieces of soft clay, however small, to harden and drop off. One by one they will, he thought. I will stake my life on the order of the fall and wait till the last one is gone.

THE NEW YEAR CAME AND WENT IN LEAD-COLORED DAYS, days spent with only a bleak exchange of words, without touch, without so much as a benign passing glance, without the other's breath felt against the face. And when it is over and the sun makes a weak attempt to alter the somber atmosphere of the season, you look back on what is only a matter of a few weeks and you cannot remember a thing. The milkman's chirpy visit thirty years ago is more vivid. The bicycle ride after school down the hill, racing a train at sunset, is more intense and immediate. The offhand, unkind comment by a primary school teacher is more memorable than anything that happened to you yesterday or the day before.

Two bodies, half dead to each other, that's what we are, thought Setsuko, lying in the bed beside Nick, who was sleeping, softly snoring in a regular rhythm, occasionally opening his mouth and sucking in a deep breath, then sighing into the air. She touched his side, leaving her hand on him, trying to recall their times together, the early days of marriage in Kyoto, sitting side by side at Entsuji Temple, fingers tightly intertwined, as the moss in the garden turned into waves that they both saw move at the same time, the walk around the Deep Muddy Pond in the north of the city, where spider-like water striders skimmed over a glassy surface, or just stopping to hold each other, just standing, doing nothing but standing together on a high bridge over the Kamo River at night. It is the beginning of summer and stiflingly hot, people are drinking, clapping their hands and singing on decks extended over the bank. But one man is dancing, arms waving in the air, off the decks that extend out from the riverside restaurants. He is continuing his routine, dancing in the air, look, Nick. But the man's friends somehow manage to grab hold of his legs and bring him from his pedestal in the air above the river down to the table, and Nick and I laugh and embrace and kiss on the bridge like there's no tomorrow. Did this all happen, she wondered, and if it did, does it have a meaning if not shared again and again by both of us? My memory, I hate its little black heart. It is as if those times had been a lie, a radiant bubble-like illusion on the surface of memory. And the worst part of it all is that touching him like this, though he is unaware of me, brings it back, lets the light of the past in again in streaks and flashes and fine lines, and when you see them you want it repeated, desperately need to have something happen now, today, something unplanned and intense that rivals it, a spark, a ray, a beam, it would take a single incident, a brilliant spot of light, to bring a thing resembling hope into the mind before the eye is cloaked over again in black.

Nick stirred, and Setsuko immediately retracted her hand. It's not embarrassment, it's fear, she thought. If he woke to find my hand on him he would turn a wall of coldness on me and a countenance more rough than the routine neglect I have become accustomed to. I wouldn't have the courage to touch him again, not even when he was asleep. Setsuko shut her eyes, and, that pall of ink settling over them, fell asleep herself.

Nick awoke, turning over to look at her. She was breathing steadily, her face perfectly still, her eyeballs not moving below her lids. What is preventing me from reaching out and touching her? What is it inside me that stays my hand as forcefully as a chain?

The two remained like that, she asleep, he continuing to gaze at her. The distance between us is an unbridgeable river, he thought, recalling the time they had lingered on the bridge over the Kamo River in Kyoto. What season was it, I can't remember for the life of me, but, yes, there was a man dancing on a table and the table itself was propped up on stilts smack in the middle of the river, teetering but not falling, and he danced there alone, sailing up high into the air, watched by crowds of ecstatic people on both banks, and Setsuko and I kissed each other but no one noticed us because all eyes were concentrating on the man leaping for dear life into the dark sky over the water.

Setsuko's hair fell across her face, her breath from barely opened lips brushing through it then drawing it into her mouth, a few strands becoming caught between her lips, her tongue licking them, trying to force them out, and Nick wanting to sweep aside the strands with his fingers but feeling that something inside him was still stopping him.

The ringing of the phone startled him and he jumped out of bed, hurrying into the kitchen, not looking back to see if the sound had stirred his wife, his mind racing over the few possible callers at 7:40 in the morning. Yuko, who had promised not to phone him at home. Perhaps someone from work for Setsuko.

"Hello, York here."

"Hello? Is that York-san?"

"Yes, Nick York speaking."

"This is Hashizume, calling from art school."

"Oh, hello, Hashizume-san. *Hisashiburi desu* (It's been a long time)."

"Oh, you speak good Japanese."

"No, I speak good Japanese clichés."

"Oh, we Japanese all speak in clichés. That is good Japanese. But, I am sorry. I call so early and wake you up."

"No problem."

"But I have very sad news."

"Oh, what is it?"

"Prof. Shiomi is dead. He died last night in his own home."

"Oh my God," said Nick, looking about the room, his eyes fixing on the half-open door to his studio.

"Terrible. He was a great, great man. I am sorry. But, York-san, are you there?"

"Yes."

"Well, this evening at six is the *otsuya* at his house."

"What?"

"Oh, I am sorry. It is in the dictionary, just a minute please. It is...here, uh, yes, an informal wake, can I say? So, you know his house where it is?"

"No, I don't."

"Do you have a fax machine?"

"Yes. My wife has one here. She uses it for her work."

"Is the same number?"

"Yes, this number."

"I will fax you the address. Please come tonight for the informal wake. The formal wake and real funeral happen later, but you must come tonight, too. It is urgent, can I say?"

"Of course I will."

"Oh, and York-san?"

"Yes."

"You have a black suit, don't you? Everybody in Japan needs a black suit, even the gaijin."

"Sure. I've got one. Yeah, I've got one."

"Wonderful! I am so happy! You know Japan so well! I will see you tonight. Goodbye, York-san."

Nick put down the receiver and once again turned to the door. Setsuko was now standing in the doorway with one hand on the knob.

"Bad news?"

"Prof. Shiomi died yesterday."

"Oh, that's terrible."

"Why? What was he to you?"

"Don't say that, Nick. He was your professor."

"You never met him, did you?"

"Met him? Yes, I went with you to Bidai, sometimes to lectures and to student parties. Prof. Shiomi was in the corridor and you introduced me once, really early, as 'my future wife.'"

"Don't remember."

"Well, I do."

Again the phone rang.

"Leave it, it's a fax," said Nick, lifting the receiver, pressing the fax button and hanging up.

The two waited as the fax emerged from the phone with a map of to how to get to the professor's home. Setsuko took it off the table, but Nick grabbed it from her, saying "Give that to me."

"Today is Wednesday, my day off, and I really need to get a perm. I'll get our funeral clothes. They're in Emi's room."

"No, don't go in there. Leave them."

"But, Nick, we will have to get them today. They'll be all smelly from being in the closet. I'll have to air them out first."

"I said, 'Don't you go in there!'"

There is nothing stopping me from defying him, she thought, I did not marry him to obey his orders. Setsuko calmly opened the door to Emi's room and slid the mirrored closet fully open. Hanging beside Emi's clothes were a black dress and a black suit, still in their plastic dry-cleaning covers.

"I should have taken these out of the plastic long ago," she said to herself, draping the two garments over the edge of

Emi's bed.

Nick stood in the doorway, fists at his sides, an expression of uncompromising anger on his face. She turned to him. I can't remember seeing him like this, she thought. Will he come to me and slap me across the face or, worse, punch me all over my body? If he does, I will walk out and not come back.

"I hope I can get into this," she said in a low voice, ignoring him and pulling the plastic off of her dress. "There is something about crape. It's ever-so-slightly rough and doesn't reflect the light like satin weaves, so it can be made to look jet black. It was perfect for *homongi* (visiting dress) in olden times, did you know that, Nick?"

I will talk about anything to him now, anything to alter that deadly expression on his face, that godawful glare, she thought. But he just stands there, unmoved, his shoulders square and raised, his head sitting on them as if he had no neck at all, his bottom teeth bared...and his eyes! They are like flames, they are burning not toward me but back into their sockets, red, glowing, little globes that will brand him.

"Nick, would you mind if I bought a new pair of black pumps to go with this?" she said, holding the dress on its hanger in front of herself and facing him. "How about you? You can't go to a wake in sneakers, you know."

Is this what is called mollifying the monster, she thought, cajoling it into a state of repose with small talk? If it is, it isn't working. His eyes continue to blaze, his fists now swaying back and forth, hitting the sides of the door with greater and greater force. Small talk will not work on the beast, she thought, the beast that is eating away the soft flesh in him with fire. I have waited long enough. Provoke it further. Stoke him. Nothing could be worse than this.

Setsuko dropped the dress at her feet, stepped over it and

pulled Emi's red down jacket off the hanger. The hanger swung back and forth on the pole until she stilled it with her hand. She stood now only a meter from Nick. It must have become dark outside, because the room itself had been drained of light and she had trouble making out his face, except for his eyes that would not look away from her. She held up Emi's red jacket to the level of his face, shaking her head back and forth in an involuntary gesture.

"Put that away," he said.

She did not budge from there.

"Did you hear me?"

She nodded that she had heard him.

"Then put that back where it came from."

Again she nodded, this time 'no,' expecting his fists, now flush against the sides of the door, to fly for her face. She raised the jacket between herself and him, as if holding it up to him, shielding herself with it.

"You have no right to touch her things. You did fuck-all for her when she was alive. It was only after she died that you started to be a mother. But to who? To what? A mother to nobody?"

All of my strength is required for this, she thought, I will not relent, I will not cry, I will not allow the worm of pity to eat its way into me. And I will not lower my hand!

"Is this some kind of trial you're putting me through? What do you want, then?" he said, taking a step toward her, tiny sprays of spit emanating from his lips as he spoke, his eyes, now molten, fixed on her. "You want to get fucked, do you?"

"Oh, don't use that word. I hate that word."

"Why should we fuck, eh? We've lost two children because of it."

How can I hold up my arms a moment longer, she wondered,

the fire that is incinerating his own body is now being propelled at me, originating at the back of his eyes, burning through them, and out, about to scorch my face, my face feeling so hot now, my skin burning. But I will not let go of this!

"There are other things in this life, Nick," she finally said.

"Yeah? Like what?"

"I don't know, like, I mean, tenderness, and love, reasons for..."

"For what? Bloody hell, for what?!"

"I don't know, Nick. I don't know!"

"Then, if you bloody don't fucking know, you have no right being in this room. It is not your room?"

"Whose is it, Nick? Whose room is it then?"

"It's hers."

"She's dead, Nick. This is her jacket. It's been in the closet, just like this, for a year and a half. How much longer does it have to stay here?"

"Did you go and see her mangled body, crushed like a pod, no body, no face left? No, you couldn't bear it. So I had to. I had to put the words in my mouth and let them out, 'Yes, this is my daughter.'"

"I couldn't, Nick. I couldn't! How much longer, Nick?"

The red jacket now blocked their eyes from each other. Setsuko's arms were stretched out, as unbending as iron. Nick was frozen by the doorway. But suddenly his fists opened, his shoulders drooped and the light went out of his eyes.

She took a step forward, the jacket now grazing his chest, but he pushed it gently away.

"All right. You have it. It's yours," he said, turning about face, entering his studio and shutting the door.

It must be pitch dark in there, she thought. He will be sitting on the floor in the middle of the room, one wall blank, the other covered now only in small fragments of clay stuck to it.

Setsuko hung the jacket back on its hanger, slid the closet closed, picked up her black crape dress and held it up, examining herself in the mirror. This becomes me. This is the only thing in life that becomes me.

NICK AND SETSUKO ARRIVED AT PROF. SHIOMI'S HOUSE A few minutes after six. The street was lined in black and white bunting, and a makeshift roofed bamboo structure stood in front of the gate. People in black were sitting in front of the gate, signing in guests, while officials from the funeral parlor were busily erecting banners of condolence along the blue cedar fence.

"Mr. York, *okusama* (Mrs. York), thank you so much for coming," said Mr. Hashizume, emerging from under the structure's roof.

"I am very sorry," said Nick, bowing.

"Thank you."

"I understand that the professor had a daughter. May I see her?"

"Yes, of course. She is inside the house. She will be greeting everyone as they pass the altar. *Okusama, mata oai dekite ureshii desu* (It's very nice to see you again, Mrs. York)."

Nick walked ahead, lowering his head so as not to bump it on the gate's lintel. The trellis, now bare, had broken into sections, and rusted nails were protruding from its edges. The house itself appeared as if a strong gust of wind would strike it down, reducing it to a heap of slivered rubble.

"I understood what he said to you. Since when did you meet the principal of the art school?" said Nick without so much as looking at Setsuko.

"I went to see him some time ago."

He now turned to her, peering into her eyes again with that fierce light.

"You what?"

He seemed so incensed he could barely speak.

"If you hate me so much, Nick, why don't you just come out and say it. Why don't you just walk out?"

At that moment two young Japanese men emerged from the house.

"Nick-san!" they shrieked in unison.

"Hello."

"Nick-san, I did not know how to contact you in Tokyo. I moved from Kyoto last year. It's Hosaka. From art university. And this is Naito, you remember, 'Installation Naito.' He collected used televisions that people were throwing out, oh, how do you say *ogata gomi*?"

"Big rubbish," said Naito.

"Yes, that's it. A big rubbish. And he used this big rubbish to make big installations."

"Of course I remember. Oh, excuse me," said Nick, stepping off the path as a very old man and woman shuffled past them, bowing.

"Well, we're both now working for Sharp. We are designing *rajikase*, you understand."

"Yeah, radio cassette players."

"Yes, that's it, you know so much."

A group of eight elderly people, all white haired, were now coming through the gate toward the house.

"Look," said Nick, "I'll see you in a bit, okay?"

"Okay, Nick-san. *Odoroita na* (I don't believe it!). You still making *chokoku* (sculpture)?"

"Yes, he is," said Setsuko.

"Oh, it's *okusan* (Mrs. York). I remember you from our parties."

"Look," said Nick, "we'll be right out."

Nick ducked into the entryway, followed by Setsuko. The smell of incense filled the air. They removed their shoes and were given slippers by a funeral official who bowed to both of them, Setsuko bowing back, noticing the corridor by the staircase, now amply lit by a tall lamp, the polished floors reflecting its light, and in a corner to the left by the waiting room the old man's wheelchair, collapsed against the wall.

The two of them followed a line of mourners into a spacious tatami room. On the altar, surrounded by white chrysanthemums and wrapped in a satin ribbon, was a photograph of Prof. Shiomi as a dapper young man, wearing a beret over a bushy black head of hair and balancing an empty cigarette holder between his thumb and index finger, a wry smile on his lips. Beside the altar sat his daughter in black kimono, bowing with her forehead to the tatami as mourners approached and planted thin, lighted sticks of incense in the sand of a vessel. As Nick came around he saw Prof. Shiomi's body lain out to one side, not in a coffin but simply prostrate on the tatami and covered up to the middle of his chest by a silk purple pall. The professor's daughter bowed once to Nick then to Setsuko, neither looking into the other's eyes nor saying a word. They filed out with others, retrieving their shoes in the entryway.

Nick's two friends from his student days were standing outside the gate, smoking by the cedar fence.

"Let's go," he said to Setsuko.

"No, we mustn't go so soon. It's wrong. You are obliged to stay and have a drink or something."

I don't have to put up with this, he thought. The old professor was my mentor, but I have paid my respects to his memory and have nothing to say to these ex-friends. I am not obliged to do anything.

"York-san," called Mr. Hashizume, approaching them. "Please follow me. *Okusama mo dozo* (Please, you too, Mrs. York)."

He went around the side of the house and through a small rickety gate, leading the two of them to a backdoor entrance, passing through the kitchen, where five or six young women in aproned kimonos were preparing food, down the corridor behind the staircase and into a twelve-mat tatami room with three long low tables surrounded by dark-green and gold floor cushions. On the tables, at each end, were trays with large beer bottles, bottle openers and dozens of little glasses.

"*Hayameshi mo gei no uchi.* How do you say that, *okusama* (Mrs. York)?"

"Oh, I don't know. The early bird gets the worm, maybe."

"Yes. Nick-san, you are lucky to have a wife like *okusama*. She is your ears and eyes in Japan, I think."

The two men sat on cushions across from each other as Setsuko brought one of the trays to them, opened a bottle of beer and poured for them. Mr. Hashizume took the bottle from her before she could put it down, gestured for her to lift a glass and poured for her in turn.

"Well, many cheers," he said, immediately downing the beer and pouring another glass for himself. "Ah, *umai* (delicious). Now, York-san, I am so glad to see you today because I want to telephone you anyway, *okusama*, please correct my English, it is so bad."

"Not at all."

"Anyway, thank you, anyway, I want to make you a delicious offer because, well, the students they say they love you, Nick-san, and some, I must tell you, quit studying when you left last year and, well, anyway, it was money for me all gone. So, Nick-san, please come and teach at my school in Shinjuku again."

"Well, thank you, Hashizume-san," said Nick, putting down his half-empty glass, which the principal readily refilled, grinning broadly at both of them. "But, I really don't know if I am such a good teacher, you know."

"You are, of course. The Yamanos, remember them? They went and lived in Italy after you taught them. You gave them inspiration. I was sad because I lost their money. But they sent me a postcard last year. They said, 'We will return to Japan only if York-sensei is teaching at your school.' Nick-san, this is a terrible situation. Please come back and save my school from bankruptcy!" Having said that, he turned to Setsuko, adding, "*Chotto ogesa desu ka ne?* (You don't think I'm overdoing it, do you?)"

Setsuko nodded, refilling his glass.

"Do I take it that you are offering me fulltime employment?"

"Oh yes, of course. Anyway, *okusama* came to me and said you needed it, so please take it."

A few mourners had now entered the room. They sat down, and started drinking and talking in an animated manner.

"My wife said that to you, did she?" said Nick, glaring at Setsuko.

"Oh yes. Excuse me, but I must greet those people," remarked the principal. "Dr. Nick, you please telephone to me tomorrow, any old day, can I say? I await you with open arms!"

He stood up laboriously from his crosslegged position and trotted over to the table by the opposite wall, bowing officiously to the people seated there, kneeling down and accepting the full glass of beer that was thrust into his open hand. Nick and Setsuko remained silent, both sipping their beer. The professor's daughter now entered the room, and all of the mourners in the room sat up on their knees and bowed to her, the women slipping off their cushions before doing so. She walked past two tables to the third, where Nick and Setsuko were sitting, and kneeled on the tatami beside them. Both Nick and Setsuko bowed to her.

"Thank you," she said in English. "You are so kind to come today. My dead father will be very pleased you are here. I am sorry that I was not able to help you when you came to me, Mrs. York. My father was so frail, only a shadow of himself in the past. He was once such a strong man, a happy man."

She lowered her head to the tatami, touching her forehead to the back of her hand.

"I am sorry," said Nick. "He was truly a great man."

"Thank you. Thank you both."

She slowly stood up and shuffled across the tatami to a group of old people.

"What did she mean about you coming to see her?"

"I came here once."

"When?"

"Last year. It was for you, Nick."

"We will talk about this later."

He has made me a promise, she thought, the promise of the threat of words, any words above silence. I am not a saint. It is not in me to tolerate an eternity of silence.

But once home he did not speak to her, except to tell her "Leave me be" before shutting himself up in his studio.

I won't Nick, she thought. I give you my promise that leaving you will be is the last thing I will do to you.

He slept that night in his studio, curled up against his spotted wall.

THE EARLY WEEKS OF 1989 PASSED WITH NOTHING TO MARK them but degrees of greater or lesser cold, today requiring a cardigan, tomorrow that coat, another day, then another, then the dreary winter was swept away by the sunlight of a false spring bringing temporary warmth. Merely a dull flow of time, he thought, and indistinguishable crowds, a monstrous swelling and you lost inside it.

Nick was being pushed along by a mass of people in the diagonal crossing in front of Shibuya Station, watching at his feet as they moved in the little space allotted to him by the crowd. Once across he turned right, passing in front of Seibu Department Store and heading up the hill toward Parco Department Store for a meeting with Yuko. He hadn't seen her in the six weeks since Christmas. "You should get more excited by things," she had told him at their last meeting, "more involved." I am involved, he thought, peering down the driveway under the church at Jean-Jean Theater, where Nakamura Nobuo was appearing in Ionescu's *The Lesson*. He neared the spot where she would be. "Even when we make love, your body is here but your heart isn't. Nick, Nick, I can never reach you!" she had told me. Reach what? There she is, Yuko standing at the Parco entrance in jeans, a white turtleneck pullover and what looks like a man's beige raincoat with the belt tied loosely in front.

"Hi," she said.

"Hello."

They walked down Spain Avenue, not speaking to or looking at each other, turned up to Tokyu Hands and continued like that past NHK until they came to one of the entrances to Yoyogi Park.

"Let's take a walk in here," she said. "I haven't been here

since I was a child."

"No, I'd rather not go in."

"Why?"

"I have my reasons."

"Nick..."

"Look. Why don't we go back to your place?"

"No. Not now."

"Oh, I see."

"It's not that. I'm finishing up my PhD and, well, really, sort of preparing to move out."

"Oh."

"I, uh..."

"Where are you moving then? Somewhere in Tokyo?"

She tightened the ends of her raincoat belt and, shivering for a moment, crossed her arms over her chest.

"No. England," she said, dropping her arms to her side.

"Oh. I see."

"I'm really not very happy in Japan."

"Neither I am, but I don't leave, do I."

"You're different. It may sound funny to you coming from me, a Japanese, but I don't fit in here. Everybody thinks the same and there is no, uh, *yoyu*...oh, what's that word? I mean, space to breathe. I feel always that I am slowly suffocating here in Japanese air. Japan is a good place if you fit in or if you can keep your head down all the time. If you are not like that, it is like being half dead all the time, walking around with somebody else's motivations in your body."

"Yeah."

"Is that all you can say, Nick? You're a gaijin. Japan's fine for you."

"What else do you want me to say? We meet, like, we haven't seen each other in weeks, and the first thing you tell me is that you're shipping out."

"You are so bound up in yourself, Nick. I wanted to tell you that before."

"And you're not, Yuko? You're not bound up in yourself, eh?"

"I have never felt so much passion with a man as I felt with you," she said, taking his hand. "Maybe I needed it to reach into you."

"Look, we can't talk about this here. It's freezing, for one thing. I want to go back to your flat."

She could not remember hearing such a direct expression of desire from his lips, not even in the early days of their relationship. She squeezed his hand, feeling a rush of warmth flow over her arms to her neck.

"Follow me," he said, leading her by the hand back to the west entrance of NHK and crossing the street to the Washington Hotel.

"Are you sure you want to do this, Nick?"

He didn't answer her. At the front desk he requested a room, put down his credit card and signed the registration card.

He shut the door to the room and began to kiss her, breathing heavily and slipping his hand under her pullover, running his palm over her breasts. She wore no brassiere. She broke away, paced the room for some seconds and sat on the edge of the bed, her chin in her hands.

"There is something that I didn't tell you, Nick."

"About your leaving? You don't need to go, you know."

"Not exactly about that."

"If you stay, I..."

He paused, unable to finish his sentence.

"I had an abortion, Nick."

"Huh? When?"

"In the middle of January. A couple of weeks ago."

Nick went to the window and, parting the curtain, looked out across the street to the west entrance of NHK. A taxi had just come to a halt and a bevy of photographers was taking flash pictures of a young woman leaving it.

"Why didn't you tell me?" he asked.

"Because...I wasn't sure if it was yours."

The taxi had swung out of the curving driveway and the photographers had dispersed. The young woman must have entered the building. Who was she, he thought. I could only see her back, not that I would recognize her. I have been living in this country for nearly ten years now and I know almost nothing about it, feel as if I am the eternal visitor, well treated by those who keep the distance of the stranger, well looked after by those who, when the spirit moves them, hesitantly approach me, bow respectfully, then shrink back, praising me for my foreign birthright, my single mark of indelible distinction.

"Nick, are you listening to me?"

"Yeah, sure."

"I'm sorry," she said, standing beside the television set, scraping the plastic No Smoking card against the top of it.

"Who's the other father then?"

"I didn't say it wasn't yours. I just said I didn't know. It could have been yours, that's all."

"Or someone else's."

"Just one person, someone I met last October at this English-speaking club thing I go to. You wouldn't come and see me. You only wanted to see me when it suited you."

"Yeah."

"He's a Japanese, but he's a *kikoku shijo*, a returnee, a Japanese who spent many years of his childhood outside Japan, so he speaks German and English and isn't at all like a

Japanese. He asked me to go with him back to England, where he's been living. He is starting up his own computer company or something in Cambridge. He's very clever. And he wants to marry me, Nick."

"Marry you."

"Yes. You are married. I want to have children, it's natural."

"Then why did you kill the one you were going to have?"

"Don't say that! It was in me only for eight, seven weeks. Minoru knows about it. He went with me to the doctor. He knows about you too, and says it's all right with him."

"It's all right, sure. It's all right with me, so?"

"Thank you for saying that." She went to him, putting the fingertips of her left hand against his chest. "I really loved you too, Nick, but love is not enough."

"Yeah. Right."

She stood on her tiptoes, kissing him several times softly on the cheek, stepped back, whisked her raincoat off the bed and rushed out. The door to the room hissed shut.

I will stand here by this window all day long, my hand lifting the curtain just enough for me to see out but allowing no one to see in, watching the people come and go at the nation's broadcaster. They will walk with engagement and self-assurance. They are not people twirling rapidly in place or reaching high into the air, they are not artists searching for meaningful intricacies in the crooked branches of a plum blossom tree. Yet, without knowing it, they too are being moved along perfunctorily, down to the last person, directed by the shape and the color of the tree, it branches and flowers, the harbingers of a new season that cute little time switches on in the brain, regulating them, making them obedient to time. I will not look at nature again, not give in to it, because I know I would be at its mercy too, and this is something I cannot allow to happen to me.

THOUGH IT WAS STILL ONLY THE 15TH OF MARCH AND SHE was not to leave the department store until the end of the month, a *sobetsukai* (farewell dinner) had been arranged for her at the Yamanoue Hotel in Ochanomizu. When she arrived at Shinjuku Station, a flurry of snow was falling on the rails between the covered platforms. She made her way rapidly, weaving through the rush hour crowd, down the stairs and out the station, wrapping her arms around her stomach and tugging up her charcoal-gray wool skirt, now much too loose for her. At least I have lost weight in all this, she thought, the holes in my belt don't go far enough around, even grief has its redeeming feature, perhaps the women who have lost children are all phenomenally thin. At this rate I will turn into one of my husband's sticklike sculptures and he will finally recognize me, his eyes will light up, his lips moisten, his hand move toward me, caress me. At last I will be the true object of his affection!

Five taxis drove in convoy from Shinjuku to Ochanomizu and up the hill to the Yamanoue Hotel, coming to a halt in front of the old cream-brick building. Their passengers were greeted by two young doormen, scurrying back and forth, holding umbrellas above the taxis' opening doors. A persistent snow was falling now, remaining as snow for a few seconds before melting into the black asphalt.

"It's around this way, follow me," said Mr. Saito, leading the group of fifteen to a side entrance and down a short flight of steps into a Chinese restaurant where they were met by the manager.

"Isetan Department Store group," said Mr. Saito.

"Yes, sir, right this way, please," said the manager, leading them to two round tables in a far corner, partially shielded from the rest of the room by a large gaudy Chinese folding screen.

Two waitresses immediately appeared with trays of beer, placing the bottles on the tables and opening six of them.

"Everybody, take a seat. Everything is taken care of tonight," said the section chief, gesturing to them where to sit, finally adding, "You are here, Setsuko-san, next to me."

Setsuko sat down with her back to the wall as the junior members of the group readily reached for the bottles of beer and poured for their senior coworkers. Arai Toshiyuki, who had ridden in the taxi directly behind Setsuko's, was seated at the opposite end of the second table. He lifted his glass to Setsuko and their eyes met for a brief moment, both of them lowering their head and looking aside at the same time. Three different waiters now arrived with trays of food, placing them on revolving disks in the center of the tables.

"There is no standing on ceremony tonight," said the section chief, drinking down his beer and lifting a bottle. "We are all equals tonight. Please, Setsuko, let me pour you a drink. *Nagai aida osewa ni narimashita* (We owe you a debt of gratitude for your long service)."

The other members of the group drank, refilling glasses for each other, holding them up to Setsuko and smiling in her direction. Setsuko lifted her glass as it was being filled by the section chief, then, taking the bottle from him, refilled his glass.

"I don't know what to say," she said. "This work has been my life in Tokyo up to now."

"That's music to the section chief's ears," piped in Tsutsui Tsutomu, who had joined the company in April of the previous year, engendering a laugh from all of them, the section chief included.

"Is that all you're going to say, Setsuko?" asked the section chief.

"I guess so," she replied, as the others chuckled once again and applauded her. "I am the one who is in your debt. Thank you all very, very much."

They clapped their hands again, raising their glasses to her.

All five waiters and waitresses, who had been standing around them with trays waiting for the nod from the section chief, now stepped forward, depositing a variety of Chinese dishes in the middle of the two tables, followed by the manager who carried a chilled bottle of German white wine wrapped in a striped blue towel. The waiters and waitresses produced fifteen large wine glasses, putting one in front of each person, as the manager poured a minuscule amount of wine into each glass, twisting the bottle ostentatiously as he lifted it from the rim. The three waiters, two waitresses and the manager remained there, standing at attention, like statues, with their backs to the folding screen, as Section Chief Saito rose, wine glass in hand, and cleared his throat.

"Everybody, once again, thank you for coming tonight. I want to propose a toast tonight to two things, if I may, to first, our dear colleague, Setsuko York, who is leaving us at the end of the month. I apologize that this farewell dinner is so early in the month, but tomorrow I am off on a business trip to Europe and New York, so, uh, and second, to the Japanese consumer in this year, 1988."

"*Bucho* (Section chief)," said Tsutsui Tsutomu.

"*Nan da!* (What is it?!)"

"*1989-nen desu, kotoshi wa* (This year is 1989)."

"*A, so* (Oh, that so). Well, be that as it may, in our country today the consumer is finally, for the first time in the long history of our country, the master of his own fate. Never has there been so much freedom in our country as today, and this at a time when in America and all over the world outside of this country there is economic failure, there are drugs and guns, child abuse, *sekubara* (sexual barassment), and, above all..."

"Section chief."

"What is it now, Tsutsui?!"

"It's *sekuhara* (sexual harassment). That's the word for it."

"What's the difference, dammit, we don't have it in our country and that's all that matters!"

Several coworkers, their wine glasses in the air for the section chief's speech, threw Tsutsui a disapproving glance.

"I'm sorry. It is inexcusable," said Tsutsui.

"Forget it. Now, where was I? Yes, well, whatever, we have no racial problems as they have all over Europe and America now, and can look forward in the coming years to greater and greater heights not only for our store but for all Japanese people, our country an escalator that knows no downward movement. *Kanpai* (Cheers)."

He drank the wine that was barely covering the bottom of his glass, and all the others followed suit.

Two hours later, Setsuko stood beside Arai Toshiyuki in front of the hotel, while the other members of the group were huddling a short distance away. Section Chief Saito, nowhere to be seen, had left shortly after the initial toast. No snow was falling, but a thin sheet of white covered the street and sidewalk nonetheless, and there was a penetrating chill in the air. Only Setsuko was to be sent home by taxi, the others walking up to Ochanomizu Station or down to Jinbocho or across to Shin-Ochanomizu Station for the train ride to their distant homes.

The taxi was idling in front of the old hotel building with its back door ajar .

"*De wa, ogenki de* (Well, take care)," said Arai Toshiyuki, grasping the top of the door.

"*Toshi-san mo* (You too, Toshi)," said Setsuko from the back seat, the automatic door closing between them. She waved to the others, the taxi started to move, and she turned to the driver, adding, "To Seijo Gakuenmae, please."

"Got it. Shall I go on the freeway to Yoga?"

"Yes, fine, any way you like."

"Got it."

In two weeks' time, she thought, I will be a free woman. My husband will become the breadwinner in the family, a fulltime teacher, and I will remain at home to look after him and myself. I will have time on my hands, time to myself. I will be able to cultivate myself, to be wholly myself again.

"I used to live in Komae," said the driver out of the blue as they were speeding on the highway above the city. "Next stop out from Seijo."

"Yes, I know it," she said, staring out the frosted window.

"Worked as a stock broker. Graduated Keio University in economics. Sold stocks to people, especially people who didn't want them, people who had money to burn, lots of that sort around nowadays. We'd take the money and use it to buy things, land, stocks, that sort of thing, for the company mostly. People'd call up, ask, 'Where's my money?' and I'd tell 'em, 'It's been invested.' Wasn't really a lie. When they called again a few months later and asked again, I'd say, 'It's been re-invested.' Never stopped like that. Never gave them their money back. Like the weasel chasing its tail. We'd just tell 'em, 'Better luck next time.' Couldn't take that game forever, though, you know. Had to do something real. Also had to leave our house in Komae. Couldn't afford the repayments on the loan. Wife's not so happy now, living out in Saitama, but I'm happy. Had to do something real, you know. Not that driving a taxi's real. It's just that now I don't have to tell people stories, you know what I mean?"

The driver did not speak to her again until they arrived in front of her apartment block, when he uttered one word, "*Tsuita* (We're here)." She signed the taxi voucher that she had been given by the section chief, filled in the amount shown on the meter, adding five hundred yen for the freeway toll, handed it to the driver, and got out of the taxi. It was freezing now, and Setsuko felt a raw chill run over her entire body, entering at the back of the neck, moving down her spine to the ends of her limbs. She shivered, her hands shaking violently, and looked up at their apartment window. No light was on. She stood her ground for some minutes before going inside, despite the bitter cold that gripped her skin, thinking, as she climbed the stairs, come what may, with each step I am going back to a time when I acted without calculation, moving agilely from one encounter to the next, from question to mystery to event, not like now when all is design, and with each step that I take, I am getting closer and closer to him.

At five o'clock, on the very same evening, Nick had left their apartment, turning off the lights, his array of sticklike figures balanced on their little rectangular bases, catching the faint light that came to the studio through the bedroom window, a gaunt army of shadows, he thought, looking back at them from the kitchen, my featureless friends, my woodyard of the insensate, my people. Listen man, you have only one step further to go, he thought. Don't go out tonight, you have no desire to. Return to your room before you too become no more than a thickened line yourself, a tangent flying off the lives of others. Flick on the lights, unroll your canvas tool holder, grasp a chisel in one hand and your sculptures in the other and carve them, shave them down, remove, shear, rid the body of its covering, pare the little sticks down to the point where one more act on them will cause them to crack, break in two and crumble or, what would be all for the better, disintegrate into a pile of dust and vanish. Telling himself that, he left, slamming the door behind him.

He arrived at Shinbashi Station some minutes after six, jogging the distance to the designated spot, the Daiichi Hotel, with his leather jacket pulled over his head. A steady fall of snow brought umbrellas out of nowhere, an acknowledged Japanese trick, he thought, in one minute an entire population is sheltered by umbrellas produced out of nowhere. I am the only person among thousands here who, running over the wet pavement, head covered, torso bent forward, resembles people battling the rain in an old woodblock print, having to defy the elements merely for the coincidence of being caught out. I will consider this angle of my body the next time I take a blade to the skin of my gaunt army.

The lobby was crammed with businessmen, bowing, shaking hands, exchanging name cards, contemplating the stiff profit of exchange, and tourists milling about in that particular tourists' daze, determined to have a good time but unsure of exactly how or where to achieve it. Nick, feeling a tap on his shoulder, turned abruptly about.

"Oh, hello, Saka-chan," he said.

"Oh, you remember my nickname. You are wonderful. Thank you very much for coming tonight," said Hosaka, one of Nick's two classmates from art school days in Kyoto. "Have you seen Naito? Too bad about Prof. Shiomi, wasn't it?"

"No, I haven't seen him."

"He's always late. Well, don't mind. He was always late in finishing his rubbish too, I mean, his installations. You see, in Japan it is a virtue to be late. Everybody thinks you are so special, important. If you are always on time it means that you have nowhere to go and you are nobody special."

"I see."

"Naito is just home in Japan from Indonesia and Vietnam. He is selling *rajikase* to Asians. It is the new market for us Japanese, I mean, new for electronics."

"You've come a long way from Paul Klee and Kandinsky, haven't you, Saka-chan?"

"Oh yes, thank you very much. That stuff was good, but it doesn't help Japan like selling *rajikase* to Asians."

"Yeah, makes sense."

The glass doors of the entrance to the hotel opened, and Naito, carrying a compact Louis Vuitton suitcase and wearing a charcoal-gray double-breasted suit, came rushing in, moving his hand up and down in a chopping gesture.

"Sorry, sorry," he said, approaching the two of them. "My plane landed at Narita at three but I made the mistake of taking the bus to Hakozaki and there must have been a car accident or something because we got caught in traffic. Nick-san, you look great!"

"Thanks. So do you, R.N."

"Oh, you remember my nickname. You are really great. So many people then called me R.N. for 'Rubbish Naito,' and it stuck."

"Now he is R.N. for Rajikase Naito," said Hosaka. "He is our number one salesman. In America he would get a big bonus. All he gets here is a pat on the back."

"You two have really gone far," said Nick.

"Oh yes, very far. You see, Nick-san, hey, let's walk while we talk, I have an extra umbrella," said Naito, opening his suitcase and producing a collapsible umbrella. "You see, when I entered the company with Saka-chan here I remembered how we studied the paintings of Jackson Pollock. Then I applied it to my sales."

"I don't understand."

"Across here," said Naito, leading the two of them through the main square in front of Shinbashi Station and down one of the narrow streets branching off it. "Action painting, remember? Well, I do action selling, never stop, always covering everything, going back to the same place over and over again and trying something new, a new approach, a new design. Eventually the customer gives in and you have a deal worth money, just like a valuable painting. You get it? Cover everything."

"Yes."

"He will be president of the company someday," said Hosaka, "and you and I, Nick, can ride on his cocktails."

"An eminently good suggestion," said Nick, smiling for the first time.

They turned a corner, entering an alley no wider than a footpath. On the left was a little restaurant, built like a country hut, with a sign above a crimson *noren* that read "Sumiyoshi."

"This means 'good charcoal,'" said Naito. "But it also means 'good life.' This is the best place in Shinbashi for yakitori, grilled chicken. And they have a sake named Sumiyoshi too, from Yamagata."

"R.N. is a *tsu* (connoisseur) when it comes to sake and yakitori."

"Oh, thank you, Saka-chan. I make you vice-president now

in charge of carrying my briefcase."

The two of them guffawed as they ducked through the *noren*, Nick following, bending nearly at a right angle to get through it himself, into the restaurant that was thick with the smoke of charcoal, burning chicken fat and cigarettes. The two insisted that Nick sit between them at the crowded counter. As he squeezed in and put the umbrella by his feet, the two Japanese simultaneously plopped packets of Marlboro cigarettes and plastic lighters on the wood counter.

"*Omakase shimasu* (We leave it up to you)," said Naito to the head cook, a youngish man with a crew cut, a *hachimaki* band tied around his forehead and a cigarette dangling from his lips, then turning to Nick, adding, "We'll start with a beer."

"Sure."

Nearly an hour of eating and drinking passed, with the two, now rather tipsy, explaining to Nick their strategy for conquering the American market "once and for all" with low-cost sophisticated electronic appliances, when Naito put a hand on Nick's shoulder and rubbed it, saying, "You know, Nick-san, I realized something very important when we all left Kyoto so many years ago."

"Not so long ago," said Hosaka. "Only, let's see, eight years."

"Eight years in an economy is a generation, Saka-chan, no, a lifetime," said Naito. "Anyway, I realized then that, well, art is sort of dead, you know?"

"Yeah," said Nick, sipping cold sake from a glass. "I'll drink to that."

"It's got nowhere to go anymore because it has been gobbled up, you know, by technology. So, Saka-chan here and I are the new Japanese artists of the 1980s, and the 1990s, and the far, far future too. You see? The future of Japan is rosy because we paint it!"

"Yeah, I'm with you."

"All that rubbish that I created at Bidai in Kyoto, it was all necessary, because it taught me that creating it was a dead end, not only for me but for everybody. All great art was created in the past. That is the definition of great art. All Japanese agree with that. Art now is just amusing entertainment."

"Yes, we do agree with that," said Hosaka, pouring sake into his glass from a ceramic jug until it overflowed and wiping the counter with his hand towel.

"So, Nick-san," continued Naito, once again rubbing his shoulder, "what have you been doing with yourself these eight years then?"

"Nothing much, just dead art. Wood."

"Wood?"

"Yeah, you know, the stuff that grows on trees."

"I didn't know that there were any trees left in Japan," chortled Naito. "All the trees that Japanese need for themselves are now in Indonesia and, sort of, places like that. Here are your trees, Nick-san," he added, holding up his pair of disposable chopsticks. "This is true Japanese art, for everyone."

"Yeah, perhaps you're right."

"R.N. is always right," said Hosaka, a jug of sake in his hand, gesturing for Naito to lift his glass and accept a refill.

"But, Nick-san, you were always the most lucky one of us."

"Lucky? Why?"

"Because you have Setsuko-san, the prettiest Japanese girl. Do you remember? You used to bring her to class sometimes and sit beside her, holding hands. Prof. Shiomi allowed it. He was very romantic. He once had a German mistress, you know, oh, when he was young. We called him 'The Professor with the Dancing Princess' because Mori Ogai, the writer, wrote a story about his German mistress like that. Anyway, you brought Setsuko-san to a party and she was so beautiful and clever. You put a rose in her hair, but Prof. Shiomi took it out of her hair and stuck it between his teeth and danced with you and Setsuko-san at the party, Nick-san. I think he was very, very drunk."

"I don't remember."

"Yes, it is true. You were so lucky. You and your wife were insera...insepra...insepara...oh, I can never say that word. What is it?"

"What?"

"The word. That word. You say it!"

Nick downed the sake in his glass and, after a pause, spoke in a whisper.

"Inseparable."

"What?"

"Inseparable."

"That's it! And then when you had your little daughter... Eri, was that her name?"

Nick lifted his glass, then put it down again.

"Emi."

"Yes, yes, little Emi-chan," continued Naito. "You were at the hospital when she was born at Kyoto Prefecture Hospital and you went racing down the street in the middle of the night, you told us, then a policeman was standing in front of his policebox and you shouted, '*Akachan umareta!* (A baby has been born!)' and he said, '*Doko?!* (Where?!)' Unbelievable! You and Setsuko-san were unbelievable, Nick-san."

"I don't remember it."

"I remember. Saka-chan here remembers, don't you?"

"Sure, I remember it."

"And did you have another baby beside Emi-chan?"

"Uh...yeah."

"A boy?"

"Yeah."

"Oh, so great! It's *ichihime nitaro* (elder daughter, younger son), the best combination for Japanese. You are so lucky, Nick-san. Saka-chan and I are not so lucky. We are miserable salarymen. Only work, work, work. Oh, we have wives and children, one each, but we never see them. We ride and ride on trains from home and always doing action selling, you see? You see, family, like old age, is something to be enjoyed later in life. The woman has her babies, so that makes her happy. We men have this life. It's great, Nick-san. This is our life now, here, in this yakitori shop. And we are so lucky, Nick-san, because the company pays everything for our fun and we have employment, I mean, fulfillment for our life, not like you gaijins. Our society protects us for everything."

"I think we leave here," said Hosaka. "Too smoky."

"Sure, I know a better place we must go to where women will sit next to us with their hands on our knee."

"Oh no," said Nick, coughing loosely into a closed fist. "Thanks just the same, but, look, I really better be getting home now."

"No! You must come with us, to talk about old days. You desire to go home to your cute Setsuko-san, I know, but she will be waiting for you, Nick-san. A Japanese man makes his wife wait. It is good. You are a very lucky fellow. *Kanjo!* (The bill!)," hollered Naito, turning back to Nick and adding, "So, how old is your little son now?"

"Eh? Oh, he's, uh, he's..."

"Must be in kindergarten now."

"Yeah. That's it."

"Does he play baseball? Pitcher, catcher, shortstop?"

Nick left the restaurant, the *noren* brushing against his face.

He ran his fingers through his hair and smelled them, kicking the snow gently with the side of his shoe, making a white row against the old wooden wall of the restaurant, evening it out, flattening it, and he thought for the first time in ten years, what would my life had been like if I had not come to Japan? What am I doing here?

HE STOOD ALONE IN A BACK STREET OF AKASAKA MITSUKE, his two Japanese classmates strutting ahead, shoulder to shoulder, arm in arm, teetering to one side then the other, slipping on the film of snow that masked the asphalt, gazing up together at the vertical rows of neon signs running up the edge of buildings like multicolored masts. Nick didn't bother to zip up his leather jacket, though the biting wind railed at him with messages, don't think that you are immune to continuing adversity, Nick, don't rest on your smug little laurels, don't huddle in your warm shelter, withdrawn, ensconced, protected. You have no protection, none at all! "Hey, Nick, c'mon." "Yeah, be right there, fellas." The buildings are so thin, like matchboxes on end, made of thickened glass, set now on strange angles to each other, listing...oooh, better hold onto this concrete telephone pole for a minute, feeling faint. "Hey, Nick, hurry please! There's this great Korean snack hostess bar up there, look!" Naito was pointing ahead to the upper floors of a concrete and glass building, Hosaka being dragged along, head cocked and prancing like a mechanical toy. "*Kankoku bijin ga takusan oru ya de*! (They got loads of pretty Korean girls there, man!)" I rest my forehead against the concrete of this pole, above a metal sign wrapped around it advertising "Kawanishi Proctologist, Go Back To Last Street And Turn Right" in English. The concrete feels somehow warming, comforting, like a hand, yet this stone-cold wind is cleaving into me, not letting me forget that, deep down, I can still feel. Why in bloody hell did they have to bring up Emi, I had put her out of my mind, ceased to imagine her with every step, I could go forward without her, but now they hold her up to me, brandish her in front of my face, and this snow, it will not stop piling up, making a thicker and thicker cover over the ground despite the fact that no more seems to be coming out of the sky. Oh yes, it will be possible, that the snow will grow up from the ground, rising into a dense white forest, reaching my knees then my waist, my belly, my chest, shoulders, neck... and I will peer over the surface of it, only my head exposed, my jaw lolling, drooping into the snow, my eyes agates, large and streaked in cream-colored waves, darting over the top, and I will see no other people in front of me, only the top floors of buildings and poles like a pin cushion of masts coursing past me, not at all like buildings but like tall ships, moving steadily on by in logical procession, the snow a swirling white sea, hiding everything alive in it from sight but my watchtower head. "Hey, Nick-san, are you okay?" They are both beside me now, lines of concern etched into their faces, my two sincere Japanese mates, upstanding blokes, action salesmen of their country's shining future, and I am clinging here to a concrete pole for dear life, my arms wrapped tightly around Kawanishi Proctologist's metal sign, will not let it go, my lips, nose and forehead flat against smooth stone, and it is warm, the pole is the warmest thing, I swear, and its warmth is penetrating my pores, through my skin, deep inside me, and I do not wish to let it escape. From now on I want to think of myself being made of it, my insides a consistently warm concrete. And maybe I can ask that this pole and my body become material that will be covered over and, eventually, unseen.

SETSUKO WAS WASHING THE BREAKFAST DISHES. ON THE table were the latest issues of *Ryuko Tsushin* (Fashion News) and *Studio Voice*. The kitchen television was tuned to *Okaasan to Issho* (With Mother). The young host and hostess of the show were dancing in a circle with about twenty children of preschool age, all waving their hands in the air to the music.

She stared at the screen for a long time, dropping the wet sponge into the sink and, wiping her hands on her jeans, went into Emi's room. The stuffed parrot, now dusty, sat on her altar in front of her photograph. Setsuko spun around and went to the mirrored closet. She opened the sliding door until the edge of the door cut her mirror image in half. She had expected the sleeve of Emi's red down jacket to slip out. It didn't. She slid the door fully open. Emi's kindergarten dresses were all there. So was the turnip costume that she had worn for her kindergarten play, hanging by its green suspenders on a wire hanger. Setsuko pushed the clothing aside, separating items, mumbling to herself. Emi's red jacket was gone from the closet.

THE PHONE CALL CAME SOME DAYS AFTER THAT, IN THE early afternoon, when Setsuko was sitting at the kitchen table, sewing a curtain for Emi's room on her new Brother sewing machine. She was watching *Tetsuko's Room*. The day's guest, Matsuda Seiko, was talking about how she had taken her baby girl to the public health center for injections. That's the same center, in Kinuta, that I took Emi to for her polio booster, thought Setsuko. And the thought came and went, without an accompanying sensation, immediately slipping from the mind.

She lifted the receiver.

"*Hai, Yo-ku de gozaimasu* (Hello, Mrs. York speaking)."

"*Moshimoshi* (Hello)."

"*Moshimoshi.*"

"Mrs. York?"

"Yes, this is Mrs. York."

"Hashizume here. From the Shinjuku Academy of Art."

"Oh, hello, Mr. Hashizume. You are always so kind to my husband."

"No, it is we here who are in his debt. The students adore your husband and, remember the Yamanos? When they heard that he was rejoining our staff, they sold their villa in Bergamo and moved straight back to Kawasaki."

"I am very happy to hear that."

"But, Mrs. York, there is something that I must discuss with you."

"Yes, of course. I will come in this afternoon."

"No, I think that we can handle this on the telephone."

"Oh."

"Uh, well, you see, your husband has come in late to work."

"Oh my goodness. He leaves our apartment quite early, in plenty of time, I am sure. Perhaps the train was delayed."

There was a momentary silence.

"Uh, yes, I am sure that he has very important matters to attend to, a man, after all, of your husband's talents has, well, has these matters to..."

"Mr. Hashizume, I apologize for my husband's tardiness. When did this incident take place?"

"Well, you see, and this is something rather hard for me to have to mention to you, believe me, I hesitated for some days before phoning. After all, York-sensei deserves the benefit of the doubt if anyone does."

"What is it, Mr. Hashizume? Please tell me."

"Well, it is not an incident. This has occurred often, in fact, ever since his joining our fulltime staff at the beginning of this month."

"He is late every day?"

"Yes. Well, his classes do not start until 10:00, so, though we require him to be here by 9:30."

"You mean, he has been missing his classes too?"

"Yes, I am afraid so, sometimes. In fact, Mrs. York, and this is rather hard for me to have to say this to you."

"Please, Mr. Hashizume, I want to know."

"Well, he has not come in today at all. We have had to cancel all of his classes. Mrs. York?"

"Yes."

"Is your husband ill or something?"

"No. I don't think so. He is fine. Every morning."

"We are extremely fond of him, Mrs. York. Please have him come to the academy on time from now on. I am asking you. Please."

"Yes. Of course. I cannot apologize enough to you. I am very sorry."

"No, that's fine. Be that as it may, I leave it in your hands. Goodbye."

"Goodbye."

She continued to press the receiver to her ear, hearing the sound of him hanging up, followed by intermittent beeps. She replaced the receiver on its hook, resting her hand on it.

"But, look at you," said Tetsuko, speaking in a rapid patter to a beaming Matsuda Seiko, who was holding up a photograph of herself embracing her baby, "you are obviously thriving in this new role as mother, and Kanda-san is such a devoted husband. Just look at that smile with perfect teeth, ladies and gentlemen, when Matsuda Seiko hears her husband's name pronounced, you'd think she'd married a dentist, ladies and gentlemen, and, well, you are amazing, combining as you do, your life…"

SETSUKO DID NOT HEAR THE WORDS THAT FOLLOWED, NOR could her eyes focus properly on the television screen. She peered into the weave of the curtain in Emi's room, trying to make out its pattern. The next thing she knew she was lying on her back in Emi's bed with her arms stiffly at her sides. She fell asleep and dreamt of Emi and herself together on a small covered boat at night, gliding over a glassy river with no reflection or shadow.

NICK ARRIVED HOME THAT EVENING AT HALF PAST SIX.

"I'm home," he called from the entryway, putting the large white Tokyu Hands paper shopping bag on the raised floor. "Setsuko?"

He picked up the bag again and walked down the hall into the kitchen. The unfinished curtain was draped over the sewing machine that was giving off a faint hum. On top of the curtain was a note.

WENT SHOPPING BE BACK SOON SETSUKO

He took a beer can from the refrigerator, opened it over the sink and was about to drink when the front door opened. He quickly went into Emi's room, stuffing the shopping bag into the closet, without closing the mirrored door.

"Setsuko?" he said, returning to the kitchen.

"I'm home," she called, appearing at the kitchen door.

"Where have you been?"

"Where have *you* been?"

"Me? Teaching. I just got back."

"Good. Then I just got back, too."

She brushed past him on her way to the bedroom. He at once returned to Emi's room, pulled her red down jacket out of the bag and hung it up, sliding the mirrored door shut. He returned to the kitchen, finished his beer and went to the bedroom. Setsuko was lying on her back on their bed, her head in her hands, elbows bent, staring at the swirling grain pattern of wood in the ceiling.

"What about dinner?" he asked.

"What about it?"

"I mean, did you get, I mean, what are we..."

"Having for dinner?"

"Yeah."

"Why don't you cook, Nick? You used to cook all the time. I recall that you were actually rather good at it."

"Yeah. I was."

"So? Right. Okay," she said, "let's go out tonight, then."

"Out?"

"Yes. We haven't been out together in donkey's years. Remember donkey's years? You taught me that in Kyoto."

"Tell me about it."

"Remember Pomme de Terre?"

"Well, all right. Let's go there tonight. Right now."

"Right now?"

"Yeah, you want to eat, don't you? Look, Setsuko," he said, taking a step toward her, his hand moving off his hip.

"What?"

"I will not ask anything of you."

"That's kind of you."

"No, stop it now. All I will ask is that you go with me to the restaurant tonight. You don't have to eat if you don't want to."

She bolted up, walking swiftly by him, through his studio and the kitchen and into Emi's room. He followed her.

"Can you tell me, please, two things?"

"Yeah, sure."

"Where have you been going every day and where in fucking hell is my daughter's jacket?"

"I don't know what you mean."

"Then say so. Nothing like a lie to break a two-year silence."

"It isn't a lie."

"No, it's ten years, a hundred years. Each day is a hundred years of misery, Nick, each and every day."

He touched her on the arm, pushing her gently aside, opened the closet and pointed to the red jacket, lifting its sleeve to show her, as if he was a merchant offering a piece of fabric to a lady.

"How did that get there?"

"It's been here all along," he said.

"Oh good, a barefaced lie. Well, that's a beginning, at least."

"It's not a lie."

She stood beside him now, close enough to touch him, pointing to the floor of the closet.

"And what's that doing there?"

"How should I know? It's one of your shopping bags. You probably stuffed it in there."

"It wasn't there earlier. And neither was Emi's jacket."

"Look, Setsuko, I..."

"Don't you touch me. Don't you dare touch me!"

"Oh my God."

"Yes, oh my God," she said, pursing her lips so tightly that the blood drained out of them, squinting angrily into his face, shaking her head back and forth.

"All right, I have been going somewhere before going to the

art school. It isn't what you think."

"I don't think anything. Go where you wish."

Having said that she ran for the front door, slipped on a pair of black patent leather dress shoes and walked out, crying in a high pitch, "Bye."

He hesitated for an instant before darting for the door himself, getting to it before its pneumatic spring shut it.

"Setsuko, stop. Stop!"

She continued to walk in the direction of the station, but, with his long stride, he was soon alongside her.

"Listen, okay, I have been going out, I mean, stopping off somewhere on my way to, um, the art school, so, look, wait, will you?"

He grabbed hold of her arm.

"Let go of me."

"No, not just for a minute. Now listen to me. Let's just continue like this to the station and go to the restaurant. It will calm us both down."

"The front door hasn't been locked."

"So what? What is anyone going to steal?"

"Your statues? Your art."

"Probably be better for everyone all around if they did."

She ran ahead now, turning the corner at Fugetsudo cake shop. He stopped short in the street and watched her run past the Ishii supermarket's outdoor parking lot and up to the light. A car horn honked and he hopped to one side, not taking his eyes off of her. But she had crossed at the light, and he could no longer tell which of the distant pedestrians she was.

Ten minutes passed and he found himself not far from the station under the cherry blossoms in full bloom, above his head a pink blanket of petals, below him only a scattering of them, random dots on a black canvas. Will Setsuko come running down this street? Will she stop in her tracks in front of me, freeze her face opposite mine, peer into my eyes, breathe onto my skin, at first lightly and then with the warm force of a wind? If only those flowers will remain for a little while longer on their branches...just a little while longer.

Nick slept again in his studio, with his back to his statues. Setsuko had come home before him and gone to bed in the middle of the day. She hadn't gone anywhere in particular, just wandered about Seijo, bowing politely to the few people that she knew who had come out of their homes to stroll under the cherry blossom trees in full bloom. By the time she woke up, he was gone.

A half-day of sleep followed without eating or drinking. There were no phone calls. The unfinished curtain had not been touched, the bathroom was only half painted, and two rolls of vinyl flooring that had been delivered by Tokyu Hands leaned against the kitchen wall. The tasks, which had seemed so natural to undertake and simple to accomplish, are now frightful obstacles to me. I am no longer able to finish anything that I start.

The next morning she heard Nick moving about the kitchen, humming a tune to himself. What is that tune? It's an Irish tune, yes, he used to sing it to me in bed when we lived in Kyoto. "When You and I Were Young, Maggie"...I hate that song! It is vile. He is about to leave. Am I able to get out of this bed? Yes, I can stand, you see, just like the next woman, no different from any other woman. I've still got my legs and they, at least, are robust. He is readying himself to go, I can tell. The refrigerator door shuts, he returns to his studio and picks up his briefcase. He throws a glance in my direction, I can see him through squinted eyes, my little coins, he is waving at me, though to him I am asleep. "Bye, Nick, have a nice day, Nick, inspire your pupils, Nick, they need you so much, go have your nice little day in the outside world." He turns away from me and returns to the kitchen. Ah, he is writing a note to me, brave little note to poor, inconsolable me, slashes of conscience on a page, warmish words that mask our banal, banal, banal tie, nothing left of it to speak of but a handful of polite words, the decorum of a dead marriage.

Thinking this, she quietly dressed herself in jeans and a wool sweater, quickly pulled on a pair of white cotton socks and, hearing the front door shut, ran to the entryway. She laced up her sneakers and followed him. He never looks back, my dear husband, walks confidently, she thought, carrying the large paper shopping bag from Tokyu Hands, strolling with a jaunty air about him, as if he was happy go lucky and free. Well, he is free, you are free, Nick York, free as a bird, free to do whatever you like for the rest of your life, I'll grant you that.

She rode the next car in his train and alighted at Kyodo, and it finally dawned on her. He is going back to Emi's kindergarten. He has something that he must do there, perhaps someone to meet.

He proceeded along the shopping street, turning the corner in the direction of the kindergarten, the bag firmly in his grip, his pace now faster, the stride of a man with a clear objective. She felt weak, her chest heaving. She kept a fixed distance from him, as if he and she were linked by an invisible taut cord, two climbers on a tall mountain.

He came to a stop in front of the kindergarten gate and she stopped too, observing him half hidden in a doorway. Were he to turn around he would certainly see me, or half of me, she thought. But he will not turn around, not now.

Nick stood below the branches of the cherry blossom tree in full bloom. I can see every depression, curve and line of this tree, he thought. I do not need to run my hand over its trunk to know the nature of the surface.

He bent down, placing the paper bag on the ground, and pulled Emi's red jacket out, draping it over his forearm. The other mothers had begun to arrive now, holding hands with their sons or daughters or simply watching them run ahead, waving to them, studying their every move as they ran away. The children do not turn back to see their mothers, nor do they respond to their words or gestures. They simply run straight for the gate, never bothering to look anywhere but ahead of them.

Nick was oblivious to those children. He stood beneath the cherry blossom tree and, as petals fluttered into the air, landing on his clothes, he began to move his feet, shuffling them at first, then lifting his heels slightly off the ground, barely moving his body, his neck swaying, his gaze fixed on the concrete animals in the yard. They are so beautiful, he thought, the little camel, the hippo and the pig, yes, perfect, really, so smooth, expressive and alive, greater now than any work of art that I can remember seeing. And, with this in his mind, he revolved about the trunk of the tree. He stared again into the yard at the large sliding glass door of the building, but the sun's beating down on it prevented him from seeing inside, instead he saw a reflection of the mothers milling on the street. They, at least, are not moving, not dancing, he thought. Only one thing has color in that reflection, it is the red jacket hanging over my arm. Suddenly the reflection disappears, a cloud is covering the face of the sun, and his eyes meet those of Emi's teacher, Miss Furui. They bow to each other, she more deeply, as he clutches the red jacket to his chest. After that he picks up the paper bag, putting the jacket back in it, and retraces his steps to the station. He passes directly in front of Setsuko without noticing her. Setsuko stays where she is in the doorway, not moving for what seemed an age.

SETSUKO UNDRESSED, SITTING IN HER UNDERWEAR ON the edge of the bed. It was late morning and sunlight was streaming into the room. She yawned and stood, opening a dresser drawer, reaching into the bottom and back of it to get an old brassiere, a pink one with a frill of lace. Her hand hit a little photo album with a felt cover. She opened it without thinking, leafing through photos of herself and Nick in Kyoto, feeling nothing in particular, no jolt, no pang, no memory. Photos of Emi as a baby lying on top of a sheepskin, her fists in the air, Emi teetering on the tatami at age one, Emi caught by the camera making her first step, Emi in her father's arms, his lips against her hair, his eyes blissfully shut, Emi in Setsuko's arms in a park, breastfeeding Emi in the old kitchen.

She turned the pages, standing by the window, coming to one of herself and Nick together on a bridge at night, kissing. Who took this photo, she thought, I cannot for the life of me recall how this photo came to be taken. They are embracing against the concrete railing of the bridge, and the photographer's vantage point seems to be in the very middle of the river itself, far above the level of human height. She shook her head, unable to explain this to herself.

Carefully, using her fingernails, she removed the photograph from its clear plastic window, turning it around. On the back, in smudged letters, were English words in Emi's hand.

Mummy happy   Daddy happy

She suddenly felt her eyes burn, covering them with her palms and weeping uncontrollably, her shoulders shuddering, her mouth opening and closing. She stopped, calm, gasping for breath, but began to weep again, this time more violently than before.

Oh my God, she thought, I did not know these words had been written by her.

Calm once again, she returned the photograph to its window, face up, replacing the album at the back of the dresser drawer. She took out her old brassiere. She sat on the edge of the bed and put it on. She bit her bottom lip very hard. At all costs I am going to prevent this from getting to me, she thought, this is only one more link in a chain, no different in size or shape from any other that determines the ironclad confines of my life.

NICK RETURNED LATE THAT NIGHT. HE HAD TAKEN TO having his dinners out, in Shinjuku, by himself. He sat at the counters of restaurants, never going to the same one twice, never speaking to anyone. What's the point of talking, he thought, why bother? At night, at home, he wished to say something to her, even reach out and touch her. I'll wait another day, he thought...just one more day.

THE NEXT DAY HE LEFT HOME AS USUAL, CARRYING THE large paper bag, in it Emi's red down jacket and, under that, his briefcase with notes for teaching. Before shutting the front door he shouted back to the bedroom, "Goodbye, Setsuko!" She didn't answer, though she was awake and aware of his every move.

The moment she heard the latch click she arose from the bed. She was still wearing her underwear and the pink lace brassiere from the day before. She went to the entryway to lock the front door.

Back now in the kitchen, she filled three glasses with water from the sink, carrying two of them into the bedroom then returning to the kitchen for the third. She lingered for some minutes in his studio. Despite having kept the apartment clean and tidy after leaving her job, even going to the extent of vacuuming Emi's room every single day, Setsuko had deliberately not dusted or cleaned the studio. His "gaunt army," as he called it, still stood in wooden formation on the workbench, the wall above it decorated in the few fragments of hardened white clay that stuck fast to it, the others having fallen away with time.

By now Nick was on his train. He had taken the semi-express and was about to get off at Kyodo Station. The train was particularly crowded this morning, and he found himself holding the paper bag from Tokyu Hands over his head. I must look ridiculous, he thought, holding this bag in the air as if it was an offering.

Setsuko was sitting on the edge of the bed staring at her dresser. Finally, after long moments in a daze, she reached out and opened the top drawer, taking out a little cardboard box. Inside the box was a bottle made of smoky brown glass.

She pushed down on the plastic child-proof top of the bottle and twisted it off. She put the bottle top beside her pillow and shook one pill from the bottle into her palm. She placed the pill in her mouth, on the middle of her tongue, and, with a drink of water from one of the glasses, swallowed it, jerking her head backward.

Nick was by now walking down the shopping street leading from Kyodo Station, just about to turn the corner in the direction of Emi's kindergarten.

Setusko shook a second and a third pill from the bottle and, putting them one at a time on her tongue, washed them down with water from the second glass. I take the pills, she thought, first one then another, they pass from my mouth to my throat so easily, oh, the third one gets caught, it just needs a bit more water, gone down now, still no change, much too early, I am self-controlled and dispassionate, and that is how I will reach you Emi, and I feel close to you for the first time in ages, Nick, I remember so well everything that we did together, I remember you from before and you are the same person now in my mind.

Nick is approaching the front gate, walking in a spirited manner, a man with a sole purpose in life. But suddenly, unexpectedly, he is stopped in his tracks, so abruptly that he nearly loses his balance and falls head over heels, his arms flailing. A little girl with a red ribbon in her hair has come out of nowhere into his path on a bicycle. One more step and he certainly would have run into her. She screeches to a stop and looks up at him, smiling.

"*Gomen ne* (I'm sorry)," she says to him, facing forward again as if it never happened and riding away.

For an instant he could not move from the spot. Then, he managed to take one step forward, and another, walking with great difficulty, as if stirring and taking steps for the first time after a long illness.

Seven pills, eight pills, Setsuko continued to swallow them, drinking water from one then another of the three glasses. "I am standing beside you, Nick," she whispered to herself. "The skin of your arm is against mine, it is summer in Kyoto, Nick, 1979, we are kissing, in public! In Japan! I love you. There is a bridge. Yes, we are definitely standing on it. It is Shijo Bridge, and we are both looking north. I love you, Nick. Emi, can you see us? We are on it! No one can ever deny that. We are right this instant standing on the bridge, Nick, you and me. You and me. Right this instant."

Nick has now reached the cherry blossom tree beside the gate and, just as he had imagined, the branches are a blaze of pink of the most exquisite blossoms he has ever seen. There is not a space between the branches or petals. There is only an uninterrupted single sheet of color and it is as if he is flush against a screen of color himself, not observing it, not able to take it in, but as much a part of it as anything can ever be.

Ten, eleven, they are becoming harder and harder to swallow, as if the throat is protesting this, I need more water, there is not much left, oh, I can't stand, can't get up, Emi, give me a hand, twelve, thirteen, ah, that's good, I feel calm now, I am on the bridge again, it is nighttime, a constant stream of people behind us, Nick is holding me tightly to him and, look, out above the river in front of us, look! He is there, that man, so tall, as if standing on invisible stilts right in the middle of the river at eye level, our eyes. And he is dancing, Nick, he is really dancing, facing you and me...fourteen, fifteen, sixteen pills...I will have to get more water, I will push these down with my finger...seventeen...eighteen...this one sticks in my throat, I gag. Get down, get down! Kiss me, Nick, kiss me and don't stop. More. Don't stop kissing me. It's a girl, Nick, our own little girl! Remember? We were together...just us...just you and our little girl...and me.

Nick is putting the paper bag on top of a blanket of petals on the ground, pulling out Emi's jacket by its sleeve, and with his feet firmly planted, he hangs the jacket on a short severed branch. It remains there as he carefully retracts his hand, fully expecting it to fall once he let go of it.

Oh, Nick, he is raising his hands high above his head, our dancing man, our river man, Nick, can you see him? He is smiling in our direction. I love you, Nick! I remember everything. There is no way that I will ever forget any detail. Nick, you are kissing me now. I feel your lips against mine and your arms around me. Nick, I love you so much. Forever. It is so warm and I can't breathe, it is so wonderful, Emi, do you know how wonderful this is? I can't...I am trying to, Nick, but I can't...I can't.

ONLY HIS BRIEFCASE IN HIS HAND NOW, NICK IS WALKING rapidly back toward the station. Entering the shopping street, he begins to jog, passing roughly through the crowd, people stepping aside to make way for him. Something has occurred to him, something that he had lost sight of. In his mind, amid disarray, he sees his statues, his soldiers, marching in place across the sky. It is a bizarre sight, but it is there, definitely real. The light in his deserted studio is suddenly blinding too, though it is not clear what the light's source is. "It must be the sun streaming in from the bedroom," he says to himself, now running, the station in front of him. "It's got to be the sun."

"I'm going back. I'm going back," he said to himself, the red down jacket hanging on the severed branch now erased from his mind.

THE WAY FROM THERE TO HOME WAS NO MORE THAN A BLUR. He opened the front door, dashing down the hall in his street shoes. He found Setsuko in a sitting position, slumped over, and when he touched her she fell back effortlessly, her neck and head dropping into her pillow like a stone.

"Oh God," he said, "Oh, Jesus," rushing through his over-bright studio to the phone in the kitchen, dialling 110. "*Kyukyusha hayaku kanai jisatsu sugu Seijo 4, 16, 301, sugu!* (Ambulance quick wife suicide now Seijo 4-16-301, now!)," he told the emergency operator.

He didn't know what to do, how to revive her. He sat on the side of the bed, holding her in his arms, cradling her as he did Emi sometimes before she went to sleep, and talking to her. She was breathing, but not responding to his words or touch.

It seemed like an age passed before the ambulance arrived, two men lifting Setsuko onto a stretcher and taking her away, Nick, still in his street shoes, following them out the front door, down the stairs and into the ambulance.

"*Okura Byoin hayaku* (Okura Hospital quick)," he said, knowing that this was the closest large hospital.

The two ambulance men, who had given her no treatment at all, could only shake their head.

"No English," said one of them, smiling. "*Gomen nasai* (Sorry)."

"*Eigo iranai. Nihongo okay. Okura Byoin ikimasu* (English not necessary. Japanese okay. Okura Hospital, we go)."

The two men shook their head again, exchanging glances, unable to explain to him in English that in Japan ambulances go only to designated emergency hospitals, no matter how far they may be from the pick-up location. The ambulance, its siren blaring, raced through the streets, Nick staring out the back window at receding cars, shielding his eyes from the glare of the morning sun, Setsuko, eyes shut, hands at her sides, still breathing, if barely.

He sat beside her bed at a suburban clinic, not knowing where he was. Her stomach had been pumped and she was resting.

"Setsuko, Setsuko," he said to her, now putting his lips close to hers and whispering. "It's me, Nick. Setsuko, listen. Listen to me. I'm sorry. I'm sorry. You must listen to me. You must come back to me. You must! Are you listening? Setsuko, I do love you. Do you know that? I swear to you, darling. I do love you. Listen to me. You must!"

The head doctor at the clinic, a very old man with false teeth and thin dyed-brown hair, entered the room without knocking.

"How do you do?" he said in English.

"Thank you. *Kanai ikimasu ka*? (My wife is living?)"

The doctor ignored his question.

"I am Doctor Igarashi, the *Incho*, or, as you say, the rector of this surgery," he said, methodically, pointing to a plastic name badge with his name written in Japanese on it. He offered his hand. "How do you do?"

Nick shook hands with him.

"My wife, how, I mean, *Kanai wa...*"

"Oh yes. You speak Japanese. Very excellent. I spent many years in your country. Where are you from, sir?"

"Ireland."

"Oh no. I have not been to Ireland. Only to the United States of America."

Nick glanced down at Setsuko, his right hand, palm up,

shaking desperately.

"I can see you are most concerned," said Dr. Igarashi, taking Setsuko's pulse. "She was swallowing many sleeping tablets. It is so fortunate that you were at home. I pronounce that she will live."

"Thank God."

"Well, yes. But, there is something that you should know, sir."

"What is it?"

"The ambulance men brought in this bottle," he said, holding the smoky glass bottle in his hand. "These are very strong medicines, you know. Your wife must have been very sad and not sleeping to take these medicines. Also, she is very thin. I hope they will not damage her brain. She should have been coming into consciousness by now, but she is still fastly sleeping. Do you know what a coma is?"

"Yes."

"She has fallen into one of those. Maybe lightly, maybe very deeply. I do not know. I pray for her speedy recovery, sir."

He once again put out his hand and Nick shook it.

"What can I do for her?"

"Stay by her side and talk to her. My experience is that these people will hear what you say, though they are unable to reply to you now."

He bowed and left the room.

MY FATHER REMAINED AT MY MOTHER'S BEDSIDE, NOT ceasing to talk to her, a steady stream of words it was, with hardly a pause to breathe. He was making up for lost time, I guess, the terrible long silence that he had maintained since my death. He wasn't even sure what he was saying to her. It was mostly those embarrassing things that husbands tell wives and wives tell husbands, or just what anybody in love with anybody probably talks about. Not having had that sort of experience in life, it's the one thing that I feel hesitant to talk about, though I'm generally pretty confident about my ability to judge people's emotions except for that, especially the emotions of my mother and father. After all, they are the two people in my life I knew the best of all.

MY MOTHER CAME OUT OF HER COMA THE NEXT DAY. SHE couldn't believe her eyes when she saw my father beside her, holding her hand. All he could say to her, over and over again, was "I'm sorry, I'm sorry, I'm sorry." She couldn't speak yet, but she smiled at him, with tears rolling down her cheeks.

NOT LONG AFTER THAT THEY WENT BACK TO KYOTO TO revisit all of the old places that they had been to when they first fell in love. They took lots of new pictures of themselves at all of those places. Someone must have snapped the picture of them holding each other in their arms on the bridge overlooking the river, just like the old one. That's one beautiful picture.

I picture myself, actually, in an auditorium, the kind you find in a lot of Tokyo neighborhoods. I am very slowly walking —almost gliding—down a side aisle. I catch sight of two people who are sitting together. Their shoulders are touching.

But I can't make out their faces at first. When I move slightly forward toward the stage, I can see that the two people are Setsuko and Nick, my mother and father.

On stage, a little girl is playing the violin. She would be about seven or eight, I guess. Her eyes are focused totally on the strings of the violin, as if they are the only thing existing, for that moment, in the world. The girl is Haruko York, my sister. You see, in the late spring of 1991, my mother gave birth to her. So she'll be nine years old when the world enters its new century.

When I think of her, which is a lot, it occurs to me that ceasing to exist isn't such a big deal after all, and that my parents' new daughter is every bit as adorable as I was, and, to be perfectly truthful about it, maybe even more so.